Morning All Day

BY CHRIS PALING

After the Raid
Deserters
Morning all Day

Chris Paling

MORNING ALL DAY

V

VINTAGE

Published by Vintage 1998

2 4 6 8 10 9 7 5 3 1

First published in Great Britain by
Jonathan Cape 1997

Vintage
Random House, 20 Vauxhall Bridge Road,
London SW1V 2SA

Random House Australia (Pty) Limited
20 Alfred Street, Milsons Point, Sydney
New South Wales 2061, Australia

Random House New Zealand Limited
18 Poland Road, Glenfield,
Auckland 10, New Zealand

Random House South Africa (Pty) Limited
Endulini, 5A Jubilee Road, Parktown 2193,
South Africa

Random House UK Limited Reg. No. 954009

A CIP catalogue record for this book
is available from the British Library

ISBN 0 09 975351 0

Printed and bound in Great Britain by
Cox & Wyman, Reading, Berkshire

For Sarah and Thomas

'I don't see what women see in other women,' I'd told Doctor Nolan in my interview that noon. 'What does a woman see in a woman that she can't see in a man?'

Doctor Nolan paused. Then she said, 'Tenderness.'

That shut me up.

Sylvia Plath, *The Bell Jar*

And so soon it will have been another day and all the secret things inside a little worse than they were and nothing much been noticed.

Samuel Beckett

PART ONE

PART ONE

ONE

Tʜᴇ ꜰʟɪɴᴛ ᴏꜰ a cigarette lighter scratched in the dark. A hand cupped the fragile flame and led a figure to the drawer where the candles were kept. When two had been lit and put one at each end of the long table the conversation – which had stopped as the final candle had burnt out – began again. At first it was hesitant, the guests were all childishly awed by the pools of candlewax spreading beneath the wicks. Then, as someone punctured the dam of one with a cocktail stick and the tiny crucible spilt its shallow load, a woman laughed and the short interlude of self-contemplation ended.

It was nearly midnight and everybody at the table was drunk, especially Gordon Meadows who could always be relied upon to be drunker than the rest. But he was a happy drunk, at least on the surface, so nobody minded. At this point he was canted precariously on the rear legs of his balloon-backed chair and saying without any obvious reference to what had gone before, '. . . I mean we live our lives driven by, I don't know, one of two . . . what's the word? Imperatives. Yes, that's it. Imperatives. What we ask of – demand of – everybody . . . is either love me – or make love to me. Isn't it?'

Having imagined that he had spoken out loud, Gordon

was surprised that none of the other seven at the table had reacted. He judged this by interrogating their expressions, the conversation having long since become unintelligible. Words and phrases reached him, occasionally complete sentences, but the meanings seemed to have become detached. When the room went dark he thought for a moment that he had blacked out.

As Gordon jolted back to the horizontal his red tie flapped down from his shoulder and flattened against his shirt front. He began plucking at the stem of his wine glass. The muddy tone produced by this introverted demand for attention was as muted as the response it provoked in his neighbours: Anne, to his left, and the quiet woman to his right were now talking across his shoulders. Previously, when he had been leaning back in his chair, they had been conducting a conversation across the corduroy peaks of his raised knees.

Then Sandy paused as she stood to pass the cheese and said, 'Oh, Gordon,' despairingly, then, 'Gordon, you do talk rubbish sometimes.' This time more warmly. The carcass of the meal she had prepared silted beneath her in fashionable and congealing fats on the uncollected dishes.

'What?' He took the cheese from her then passed the cold marble slab on to Piran. 'What!' Being a teacher, Gordon was unused to being patronised, however fondly, although it was something he'd recently been aware of happening more often. It was almost as if people no longer knew how to take him. His wife, Miranda (ironic, smart, lovely Miranda), accused him of being depressed; a charge he vigorously denied, although when he examined the accusation he began to wonder if there wasn't some truth in it. He rarely said anything nowadays that wasn't targeted to elicit a specific reaction.

'Don't get the hump, Gordon.' Piran's lighthouse beam of conviviality swept round the table.

'No. Let him. Just, I mean if he wants to, just let him.' Sandy looked at Gordon, watching for a reaction, then craned her neck a little forwards to provoke one.

'Oh piss off, I know when I'm . . . well, you know.' As Gordon focused his attention on spearing a piece of ripe Brie, Sandy and Piran exchanged a married look which instantly transmitted numerous pacifying messages between each other. Gordon's Brie clung briefly to his knife then fell and landed like a huge tear among the crumbs on the white cloth. He had reached the stage of inebriation at which hand/eye co-ordination fails just as the mind begins to believe it has, once more, achieved sobriety.

'I'm sorry, Sandy . . . I really am.' Gordon set about scraping it off with the blunt edge of his knife but the mucous residue adhered to the linen.

'It doesn't matter, really.'

'Look, let me have a bash at . . .' Gordon dipped the corner of his stiff napkin into a glass of mineral water then began rubbing at the cheese stain. The cloth ruched and set Gordon's wine glass wobbling. He lunged for it but it had already toppled and his action served only to dash red wine efficiently and exclusively into Sandy's lap.

Seven mouths clamped shut. Only Sandy's remained open, gasping in shock. 'For Christ's sake! It's Hamnett. Don't you understand, Gordon, it's a Hamnett . . .'

She rushed from the room calling for the au pair. Gordon glimpsed the young Swede, antiseptically blonde and swaddled in a long black sweater, emerge unperturbed from the burrow of the basement kitchen. She followed Sandy up the stairs carrying a crispbread like a laboratory slide in her improbably long fingers.

'Did she say Hammamet?' Clive said after a reasonable pause. Clive was the oldest of the eight friends grouped at the table but looked the youngest. He had shiny hair, and, for a forty-three-year-old, too much of it for Gordon's liking. He also possessed an energy and an undimmed enthusiasm for life, neither of which Gordon seemed to have at all. On top of all that he also still had a chin and a waist; he was as lithe as the player-manager of a football team, the profession whose dress code he seemed to have adopted. Tonight he was wearing what used to be called 'slacks', grey slip-on shoes and a pastel-pink sweater that clashed with his perpetual tan.

'No. She said Hamnett,' Piran said, though he'd known little of the label until he'd discovered the damage his wife's purchase had done to their joint credit limit. He waited for Gordon's response. Gordon, being a teacher, knew a little about quite a number of things but not much about anything in particular. Clive's long suits were 'footy' and what would be classified under the 'entertainment' category in a pub quiz. Piran's extensive classical education equipped him for *The Times* crossword but otherwise qualified him for young fogeydom and much red-brick ribbing.

Gordon floated, 'That would have . . . ah . . . I imagine cost . . . well . . .'

'The best part of a thousand,' Piran sniffed, shoving his chair back. The bare varnished floorboards squealed at the friction burn. 'Anybody for a brandy? Not you, Gordon, of course. You've had enough.' As he left the room the candle flames looped in his wake then knotted tight to their wicks. Cartoon versions of his broad profile were thrown against the walls. The dining room was in the midst of re-decoration; the paper had been stripped to the line of the high picture rail leaving the walls plaster bare. But nobody commented on it for fear that the room was, indeed, finished and Piran and Sandy had opted for a minimalist interior designer.

Gordon continued to toy with the stem of his empty glass. He was sobering rapidly and he knew the journey home

6

would be hell. He hadn't been able to look at Miranda since the spillage but his shin was still aching from the sharp kick she had delivered to it under the table.

'Only we went to Hammamet last year,' Clive went on with his habitual enthusiasm. 'Tunisia . . . bloody fantastic place. Fantastic. Clean? You wouldn't credit it. Fantastic people. Absolutely salt of the . . .'

'You hated it.' Anne said heavily. The more annoyed she was with her husband the clearer her enunciation always became. She was posh, he was not. The gulf widened at moments of crisis and came to matter in a way they could normally pretend it did not.

'Did I?'

'Yes, you said it was a "shit-hole".' She handled the word with silver tongs. 'You moaned from the moment we arrived.' She redistributed her operatic frame on the flimsy chair.

'Did I?' Clive added a thoughtful 'Ah,' then inverted it so that it became a truncated laugh. He hadn't the energy for a full-scale row so he watched his wife carefully for clues to his retreat.

Anne leaned back from the table and acknowledged her victory with a smile. 'He always forgets. Sometimes you'd think we went away so often that . . .' She drew hard on her cigarette, her gigolo pleasure, then vented the smoke from the corner of her mouth. They had all smoked and now only Anne smoked. Clive and she had been left behind in many ways, but her cigarette habit was the most telling. At least Piran and Sandy still allowed her to smoke. That was, at least, something. '. . . I don't know. You're thinking about Portugal, darling. We loved Portugal, you hated Tunisia.' The 'darling' was a concession. The tension diminished.

'Portugal. Yes, course it was Portugal.' Clive said, visibly relieved. 'Brill. Absolutely . . . brillo.'

Of course Anne knew that it wasn't Portugal and it wasn't even Tunisia, but every holiday was such torture that any comparison was unhelpful. Anne took pleasure in nicotine and gin and golf but not in Clive. Clive took pleasure in Sandy (now upstairs, while the au pair dealt with the stain on her dress) and his work, his footy and his car, but not in Anne. Communal time was not happy time.

Anne had lost her looks early. Gone to seed, as Clive confided to Gordon one night. Even the sex hadn't lasted long beyond their courting days in open-topped cars. But then sex never lasts and now Anne had put on a huge amount of weight and sailed through the world on a galleon of swirling prints. It was hard to imagine how much flesh tensed the billowing sails because her face retained the blush and angles of a teenager. Clive had pretty much given up on his sex life until one night he had discovered Sandy's hand in his trouser pocket. Unshockable Gordon was shocked when Clive told him this. Sandy, he had always assumed, was too unhappy to be having an affair, though, on reflection, he wondered whether it might, of course, be the affair that was making her unhappy. Gordon wished Sandy would confide in him as she had used to do. But the time would come; they went back a long way.

So Clive and Anne were still together – just: materially the most successful of the four sets of friends at the table, if lagging behind in the envy stakes. Clive leased a large warehouse on an industrial estate from which he operated a wholesale car battery business. It was lucrative, but as far as the rest of them were concerned it was dirty money, reeking, as it did, of inflated garage bills, wads of oily fivers shoved deep in the pockets of greasy overalls, 'Anything off for cash?'

Piran's remuneration as a barrister meant that he and Sandy were more than comfortably off. And Gordon and

Miranda lived on his teacher's salary supplemented by her occasional earnings as a freelance illustrator (she did calendars, but she had high hopes for a new range of wallpapers). They were the most envied of the couples, but envied by the others for something they had no influence over: a sense of purpose and unity. What gave them a sense of unity was their children – and children, as Gordon argued, provide their own sense of purpose: that purpose being to protect them for as long as possible from a world designed to rob them of the credentials that allow them to practise as children.

The other two at the table were neighbours of Piran and Sandy and were known in private as the 'quiet couple'. The woman worked in publishing and her pale but charismatic husband was a writer. They were called in to make up the eight and cropped up occasionally at parties, tolerated but marginalised. They also shared a sense of style which eluded the rest of them, and were used by the others as expert witnesses in discussions on the arts. It was the quiet couple who wore the first deconstructed suits. Then, when Clive arrived one day with an Armani jacket over his Pringle sweater, the quiet couple had re-discovered formal tailoring. They were currently going through a linen phase with close-cropped, dyed blonde hair, white T-shirts and John Lennon glasses. The woman looked tanned and Californian in a Hockneyish way, the man more East Coast and Warholishly consumptive.

Gordon avoided further discussion of the merits of the Algarve by following his host down into the kitchen. He was never entirely sure when Piran was joking but, at that moment, he needed a brandy more than he needed anything. He found Piran bent at the waist, peering closely at the work surface. For a fleeting moment, Gordon wondered whether he was having a heart attack and racked his brains for details of resuscitation and the recovery position. But Piran seemed to be sniffing. His broad waist, barely constrained by his green striped shirt, was undulating above his trouser line. His buttocks clenched, then he raised himself suddenly back to his remarkable full height with a stifled but satisfied roar. His unfashionably long hair, in the midst of a seasonal change from the dull blond of autumn to the cold grey of winter, settled again to its precisely sculpted helmet.

'Piran?'

Piran span round. A five pound note was rolled like a cigarette between his fingers; he brushed his shirt sleeve quickly across his nose. The habitual calm was gone from his eyes. He looked like a man who had thrust his head from the window of a speeding train.

'Yus,' Piran said nasally, flexing the frozen muscles of his cheeks.

'Good God.' Gordon found himself recoiling. 'Is that what I think . . . I mean it's not . . .'

'Go-caine? Yus, it's cocaine. Trying to look after the old liver for a few weeks.' Piran patted his liver fondly. 'Now where has that stupid woman put the brandy glasses?' He wrenched open a glass-fronted kitchen cabinet, slammed it to the earthquake rattle of expensive crystal, then searched the cupboard below. 'Don't gape, old pal.'

Gordon tried not to gape. 'Isn't it just asking for it, taking that stuff . . . I mean being a . . . what if you got . . . you know?'

'Where do you think I get the stuff: Waitrose?' Piran stormed, but seeing Gordon's look of concern he backed off. Gordon was, of course, about the only one of his and Sandy's mutual friends he had any time for: a man who clearly needed protecting. Not so much from others, but from some of the more unpalatable truths of the world. Piran proceeded more gently. '. . . No, you see, we have a discreet and reputable supplier who comes to Chambers. He's an extremely enterprising young man. He even has handbills he printed on some bloody government ah, good, retraining scheme.' Piran pulled out the brandy balloons, four bunched in each huge hand, sniffed them, then poured eight generous measures. 'He has one of those old-fashioned butcher's bikes – do you remember them? – you know, big black frame, basket up front. It looks completely legitimate and it has the added advantage of providing him with somewhere to put his scales. He masquerades as an executive sandwich seller.'

'And you trust him?'

'Yes, we have enough on young Seaman to put him away for a very long time. Mutually Assured Destruction. It's quite safe.' Piran sniffed again and tested his tingling gum with his index finger. 'Would you like me to procure you some?'

'No. Thank you. No thanks. I'll stick with the . . . ah . . .' Gordon waved hopefully towards the tray of drinks.

'Of course. Oh, I seem to have poured one out for myself.' Piran drained a glass then Gordon followed him back to the dining room where he found Miranda drawing sensually on a cigarette and giving Clive her narrow-eyed Mata Hari look from beneath her immaculate fringe while Anne looked on smugly and said, 'It wasn't me darling. She begged me for one.'

'Pathetic. No will-power whatsobloody ever, Miranda.' Miranda stared him out and Gordon slumped glumly onto his seat. He knew that if he didn't get a drink within the next two minutes his alcohol level would drop below the point at which a single measure would be of any use to him. But then Piran leaned towards him and he found a chalice of brandy glowing before him on his place mat. He cupped the glass and sloshed the viscous liquid round the bowl. Then he downed it in one.

He had another brandy. Then another, and Miranda had

another cigarette to even things up, but Sandy never re-appeared so when Gordon went to the lavatory he timed it to coincide with the visit of the quiet woman.

'Oh, sorry . . .' he mugged as they reached the lavatory door at the same time, 'No, you first. Please. I'll use . . . ah . . .' Gordon pointed upstairs.

'You don't even know my name, do you?' The woman stood with the knob of the lavatory door in her hand, flicking the brass lock cover with her perfect thumb-nail. She was drunk, but more in control of it than Gordon. This cut against one of Gordon's favourite stereotypes. Women approaching middle age, it seemed to him, became more adolescent and carefree when drunk whereas men became more maudlin and weighed down by their responsibilities. Piran posited that this was because men's conditioning never let them forget their primary role as providers, while a woman's traditional role of reproduction, once achieved, left them free for self-discovery. Gordon shot down this theory on the grounds that it was the women who had escaped having children who were the most often randily and raucously pissed. Gordon couldn't remember what Piran had come back with but he said to the quiet woman, 'Of course I do.'

'What is it then?'

'It's . . . ah . . .' He stopped as she smiled, waiting to be teased. Demanding it. But he had forgotten the question. 'I'm sorry, what did you say?'

'I asked you what my name was.'

'Of course you did.' Her frankness had wrongfooted him. 'Don't you trust me?' he said.

'Trust? . . . heavens, Gordon, you do give yourself away, don't you?' She opened the door on the pine-fresh room. 'Tell me though . . . what are you up to at the moment?

How are you doing? I mean Piran's always talking about the courts and Clive his garage . . . battery thing.'

'Wholesale battery business. He makes . . .'

'. . . a mint.' They laughed together at their mutual recognition of Clive's stock phrase. 'Yes, whatever. But you never say anything.'

'I thought I did.'

'No. You offer nothing. It's rather sinister. It's also unfair. You have nothing to regret the next day and you skulk off with all our secrets squirrelled away in your rucksack.'

'Rucksack?'

'Yes. I don't know why I said that. Strike it out.'

'Well does it matter? What does it matter how I am? I mean it matters who I am. Yes, that matters. Certainly it does. But how I am . . . I mean does anybody really . . . care?' Coming round a blind bend on the other part of his life, Gordon found himself veering dangerously towards despair.

'I don't know, do they?'

'Well . . .'

'They can't do if you feel they don't, I suppose. But it's rare to find a man of your age who isn't, I don't know, going on about himself or his bloody job all night.'

'But who I am,' Gordon slurred. 'That's. Christ, I don't know. But you know what I . . . I mean, what about the quiet, ah, I mean your husband. I mean, do you include him in that?'

'Oh, I don't know. I never meet him socially. I suppose he's a listener rather than a talker. I imagine he seems dull. Or sinister. Or both. But he never talks much. At least that's what I'm told. Some of my girlfriends fall for it. It can seem like wisdom. I think it's just . . . fear.'

'Fear?' Fear was something Gordon understood.

'Fear of giving himself away. I suppose when you spend all

day making up beautiful phrases the real world must seem terribly . . . mundane. Clumsy.'

'Sinister.' Gordon said.

'Yes?'

'You said "sinister". Again. About him. And about me.'

'I'm sorry. I don't have my thesaurus with me.'

'No. I wasn't . . . I mean, I'm not trying to . . . it's old-fashioned. An old-fashioned . . . concept. Isn't it? Jack the Ripper. Gaslight. London fogs. Hansom cabs. Bedlam.'

'Are we doing word association now?'

'No, I'm just trying . . . oh, God. I don't know.'

'No. I'm sorry.' She laid a healing hand on his arm. 'The simple truth is that I must have read it. Seen it. I've been working through my slush pile. If you want to know about sinister you should take a look at the tower of A4 in my office. Sometimes I think I ought to get some of the manuscripts biked straight round to Scotland Yard. What were we talking about?'

'The world. Being sinister.'

'Yes, of course we were. I know, it was Peter. Something he's writing. That was it. He read me the opening of his new book. I think he's a bit stalled with it. The Sinister . . . something. Look, sorry, I must use the loo.' The quiet woman closed the door behind her. Gordon waited until he heard the sigh of a zip, then he went upstairs.

The stairs of Piran and Sandy's house are Piran's, the rest of the house, Sandy's. The arrangement was arrived at soon after they moved from their flat in the Temple. Sandy, it was agreed, would do the rooms and she would allow Piran the stairs for his big hunting prints. To Gordon's eye there seemed to be fewer of the heavy, black-framed pictures than there were before, but the Bickleys' stairs were always climbed with a distinct feeling of claustrophobia. Hounds pursued foxes which pursued hounds which, in turn, jumped frames only to be pursued by armies of blood-red jackets. Climbing the Bickleys' stairs always put Gordon in mind of that film by Roman Polanski in which Catherine Deneuve was molested by arms protruding through the walls of a corridor.

Gordon was thinking warmly of Catherine Deneuve when he heard Sandy's voice from a bedroom. She didn't sound angry any more so he went in without knocking and found her sitting on the bed, naked except for a pair of translucent knickers. The au pair was standing at the foot of the bed with Sandy's dress draped over her arm.

'Oh. I'm sorry,' Gordon said, swallowing his tongue. He felt a pinch in his chest and a glow in his groin. Women's bodies would never cease to come as a shock to him. A pleasant shock, but, a shock none the less. They were so much more complete than men's and there was also so much more of them. With a man, Gordon reckoned, you pretty much got what you expected when he stripped off. With a woman a couple of hundred years of couture and corsetry made it almost impossible to pre-judge the weight of her breasts or the fullness of her waist. Gordon realised he hadn't seen Sandy naked for more than fifteen years, and she looked none the worse for it. Better, perhaps, unlike he, who looked two stone worse.

'Would you like a photograph?' Sandy crossed her arms but made no other move to cover herself up.

'If you wouldn't mind.' Gordon sat down on the bed. The au pair looked at him and laughed, showing a set of perfect teeth. Then she took her half-eaten crispbread with her and left the room. Her leaving immediately compromised them and Gordon jumped up again.

'Relax, Gordon.' Sandy patted the bed. 'Relax. Nobody's going to come up here. And if they do I can pretend I'm still cross with you about my dress. I mean it's not as though you've never seen me starkers, is it?'

'Well, no, of course. But not since, you know.'

'You married Miranda. Well that rather speaks for itself, doesn't it?'

'Yes.' Gordon sat down and relaxed a fraction. Sandy leaned across him and he found her nipple in his ear.

'Hwm i mke peol ly mi?' Gordon heard.

She straightened up, fingering a half-smoked reefer back into shape from her bedside ashtray.

'What?' he said.

'Do you have a light?' Sandy's thumb toyed with the cardboard roach protruding from the end of the joint.

'No. I don't smoke.'

'Bugger . . . what I said was, how do I make people like me?'

'. . . I could get you a light . . . from Annie.'

'Don't want it now.' Sandy tossed the butt end petulantly towards the wastepaper basket. It missed and landed in the overspill of the velvet curtains, among the debris of lipstick-kissed tissues, charred green joss sticks and fragrant cotton balls. 'Oh I know, Gordon,' she sighed, 'I know . . .'

'Do you?'

'Yes.'

'Good . . . good,' he said, having only the vaguest notion of what she was referring to. Gordon lay back. Sandy leaned over and her breast brushed his cheek. He resisted the contact.

'Touch me,' Sandy said.

'What?'

'Touch me. Touch my breasts. You want to, don't you?'

'No. Don't be . . .'

'What?'

'Well, for heaven's sake . . .'

16

'Oh come on, Gordon, be a grown-up about it.'

'I was trying to be.' Gordon reached up to cup Sandy's breast in his right hand, then, with a little gentle pressure from his thumb, teased out her nipple.

'Are you happy?' Sandy seemed suddenly to lose interest. She knelt up on the bed and rounded on him, her breasts lagging a split second behind. Watching them settle to equilibrium, Gordon immediately forgot he had been asked a question.

'I mean really happy?' Sandy had taken his first silence as assent.

'I suppose . . . well . . .'

'I'm not.' Sandy glared angrily over her shoulder at her image in the mirror. As Gordon began again abstractedly to stroke and mould her breasts she watched the other woman catch her breath and arch her back. 'I'm not happy with Piran, that's for sure. I'm sure he's sterile. Which is probably a blessing in disguise because his family are all stark raving mad. All of them. His mother's a simpering idiot who's always telling him how wonderful I am. His brother's . . . I don't know, I think he owes us money. And Pops . . . Christ. Completely gaga.'

'I met him. At the wedding. He seemed alright . . . beautiful house.' Gordon wondered whether he should stop what he was doing to Sandy. It felt furtive. But as the logic of seduction pursued its natural course he was now involved in exerting a more strategic pressure for a more particular response. To have stopped would have been difficult, not to say impolite.

'That was ten years ago. Anyway, the place leaks like a sieve . . . total liability. We went down there last weekend and I caught Pops wanking.'

'Yes, well, I suppose we should applaud, shouldn't we? I mean he must be knocking on a bit . . .'

'At the table. Over dinner. Christ.'

'I see.'

'And Clive . . . well . . . he's such a . . .'

Gordon's interest perked up. 'Yes?' It was too easy. By ignoring his teasing hands, Sandy was making it too easy for him.

'I can tell you, I suppose. He might make a mint but he's such a premature ejaculator. I mean I only have to touch him and it's out with the tissues and the post-coital fags.'

'I thought he'd given up.' Learning that Clive still smoked was somehow more shocking to Gordon than hearing of his sexual inadequacies.

'Yes, we've all given up, Gordon, publicly, anyway. If I didn't fancy him so much I'd tell him to piss off back to his battery shop . . . you won't tell him, will you?'

'Well . . . of course n . . .' Gordon's palms were now lightly rubbing Sandy's back and waist, travelling higher and lower until his fingers found their way inside the elastic of her knickers. She acknowledged his attentions by deftly slipping them off. His fingers found a cleft of warmth which gave to his touch and became a thread of moisture. Sandy breathed harder.

'Men don't talk anyway, do they? I mean I should have listened to Anne . . . Perhaps I did listen . . .' Sandy caught her breath again, this time, as Gordon read it, clearly indicating her mounting interest in his attentions, '. . . listen to Anne. Yes, I suppose I . . .' a sigh this time, stifled, but a sigh of pleasure, 'must have listened to Anne because she was always going on about how good he was . . . well, women talk, don't they? Please don't stop doing that. Sometimes if men only . . . but we were happy together weren't we?'

'Us?'

Sandy's right hand was reaching beneath her to unzip

18

Gordon's fly, a task made difficult by the pressure against it. 'Yes. Us.'

Gordon nodded. Insofar as he was still capable of thought, he was thinking just the same thing. But Sandy didn't laugh much now. And neither, Gordon realised, did he. Sandy's fingers tousled the short tangle of hair at the base of his stomach. 'What are you thinking?'

'Nothing.' Gordon was now almost incapable of thought. A purple pressure built inside his brow.

'You look so sad, my darling . . . Sometimes I just want to put my arms round you and make it all better for you.'

'Do you?' Gordon enjoyed the poignant novelty of concern.

'I thought you . . . well, of course you must know how we feel. Not all of us I mean . . . or perhaps you don't.' Sandy's nails were tramlining the inside of Gordon's thighs.

'God . . . God.' Gordon stretched out and back across the duvet. Sandy straddled him and her face eclipsed the dimmed ceiling light. Then he felt her lips on his, her tongue between his teeth, tasted their saliva commingling. The years fell away as he felt a genuine joy rise within him. He eased her hips above his, then leaned upwards until they were locked together.

They arched in complicit ecstasy, beyond speech and thought, and neither of them noticed when the quiet woman poked her head round the door. She watched them for a while; fondly, like a mother watching her children playing in the sand. Then she clicked the door shut and stood guard in the corridor.

'Mmmm . . . that's nice,' Sandy said as they finally broke apart. 'I love your lips. I always loved your lips. Nobody has lips the same weight as yours.' She lay on top of him, her head against his breastbone; a welcome ballast preventing him rising from the bed. 'Now say something nice to me.'

Gordon hesitated. They seemed to have reached a moment where the difference between honesty and kindness could change their lives completely. But it was honesty that had first driven them apart: his sullen, painful, uncalled-for admission that he had slept with Miranda. But honesty now . . . he ranged through what he felt and was depressed to find that he no longer knew exactly what he felt. His life had become as confused as his politics, his thoughts as furred as his veins. Even black and white now carried associations that cried out for qualification.

'Don't worry, Gordon. I'm not asking anything of you.' Sandy sat up and padded to the wardrobe; on her back she wore the blush of a spent passion. She drew out a short black dress and hung it against herself. 'What do you think?' She pirouetted coyly.

'I think . . . I think you'd look beautiful in anything.' Gordon settled for honesty. Or was it kindness? Sandy dressed and Gordon went to the lavatory.

Sometime later, when they went back downstairs and walked into the dining room together, Gordon discovered his fly was still undone. Miranda spotted it immediately and pointed it out loudly to the table at large, but it was a measure of how Gordon was perceived that nobody but the quiet woman gave it a second thought when he announced he'd just had forty winks on the lavatory.

TWO

'So you'll take them, then?' It was the following morning and Miranda was making up in the hallway mirror.

'Take them? . . . Good God!' At her shoulder Gordon was doing up his tie.

'Whooat?' Miranda halted, her lipstick poised an inch away from the oval of her mouth.

'I've done it . . . look.' He positioned himself behind her so that she could see the reflection of his tie in the mirror.

'Oh, you've tied your tie, Gordon. That's marvellous. Now perhaps we can have a go at teaching you to do up your shoelaces.'

'It's a Windsor knot . . . and the pattern, you know, the stripy bit is in the middle of the knot.' Gordon, to Miranda's constant irritation, had never quite lost his childish glee over minor triumphs.

'I haven't got time for this.'

'Sorry.' Gordon backed out of her eyeline and stepped on something which immediately scuttled away like a mouse. It was Ben's foot. Ben howled and scooted off towards the kitchen on his tricycle. He was wearing a yellow fireman's helmet and his pyjama jacket, but was naked from the waist down. Ben had been disturbing their sleep for two years and eleven months. He had dark hair, immense brown eyes capable of expressing a range of emotions that Gordon constantly marvelled at, and a beauty that was most evident to other people or when he was asleep. He lived in the shadows around the skirting boards, reaching up only to just above Gordon's knee. But, for such a small thing, the disruption he caused to the household far outweighed his size.

Ben had just discovered his penis, which he inspected and displayed at every opportunity. Gordon and Miranda had long, fraught conversations about Ben's penis habits. Miranda was convinced it was a sign of things to come, while Gordon tried to point out that if women had penises they'd probably spend as much time touching them as men did. Probably more, considering the amount of time they habitually spent examining, patting and re-positioning parts of their body. A penis was, Gordon argued, a wonderful thing: a constant, sluglike companion which gave you direct nerve access to most other parts of your body. It was the forerunner of the diagnostic computers you now found in high street garages; those that delivered an immediate readout once they were plugged into the engine. It was at this point that Miranda called him a sad wanker and went to bed muttering about how, for women, everything was on the inside. Everything.

What Miranda didn't know was that, having discovered his own penis, Ben now stalked Gordon with the sole intention of getting a glimpse of his. Unless he remembered to lock the lavatory door, Ben's face usually appeared from behind Gordon's right knee or, worse, between his legs the moment he was unzipped and standing over the bowl.

Miranda said, 'You're taking Ben to Margaret's and Penny to school.'

'But Penny walks to school.'

'She does, yes, but as I think we discussed last night, she has games and good work assembly and she has to take something electrical in to be . . . dissected. You said you'd take her.'

'Oh . . . fine. Of course.' Gordon gave in to the rising inflection.

'Penny! Five minutes.' Miranda went searching for Ben in the kitchen but the back door was open and she discovered a trail of his footsteps across the dewy lawn. He'd stopped beside the stone birdbath where he was poking at a pile of fresh cat excrement with a bamboo cane. Miranda upended him and carried him under her arm like a rolled rug to his bedroom. There she fought and quickly won the battle to get him dressed while he continued his tirade against being despatched to the child-minder's. She silenced him with a kiss which he wiped away with the back of his hand then smiled brightly, pointed at his new clock on the wall, and said, 'Sixty-five.'

'Twenty past eight, darling,' Miranda corrected gently. 'Time to go.'

'Don't like frogs.'

'No. There aren't any frogs at Margaret's.'

'Not going Margaret's.'

Ben followed her downstairs then went into the lounge where he began rummaging through his pile of videos. He emerged, smiling broadly, with a tape bearing the face of Charlie Chalk, but there was nobody around who could insert it into the machine so he sat on the settee, pulled a cushion to his chest for comfort and dropped instantly to sleep.

'More cat shit on the lawn. Don't forget Penny's lunchbox. Tell Margaret I'll be back at four. Ben's sandwiches in the fridge. One packet of crisps each. Don't worry about putting the washing out. Bye.' Miranda kissed Gordon on his cheek and he watched her rummage for her keys as she tugged the front door shut behind her. For the first time that morning he was aware of how beautiful she was. He took her beauty for granted, perhaps even fearing it, believing, as he did, that she dressed for others, never for him. The dress she had on today was indecently short – even for a meeting with a potential buyer of some of her designs. He knew he hadn't seen it before because if he had then he'd certainly have remembered.

'Pen. Two minutes,' Gordon shouted up the stairs. Penny emerged behind him from the kitchen, with her lunchbox, her sports kit, a large plastic bag, and her coat on. 'Two minutes, Pen,' Gordon repeated redundantly, glad of Pen, wishing he knew more about what went on in her mind.

'Ben's asleep in the lounge,' Penny said wearily.

'Right.' Gordon laid his arms on Penny's shoulders. 'I love you, Pen. You know that, don't you?'

'Yes.' She looked up at him, willingly bearing his weight, waiting for the catch. Tears pricked her eyelids.

'Good.'

Love was a currency that had been sparely traded in Gordon's childhood. An invisible import. Implicit but tricky to quantify. Gordon told Pen he loved her whenever he could. But only when they were alone. He rarely told Miranda that he loved her, even though he did – in a way. The word felt old with Miranda. Corny. Her irony tarnished everything.

'You're not going to die are you, daddy?'

'God, I hope . . . why do you ask that?'

'You look sad. That's all.'

'Of course not.'

'Or leave? Claire's father left.'

'No. I'm not going to leave. I promise.' But he was, of course, one day.

Penny trailed patiently back to the kitchen and turned the radio on. The nihilistic thump of rap triggered a death in her eyes. Gordon watched as the music tripped out her attention like a circuit breaker. Penny, for as long as he could remember, had always been able to see through him. She was ten years old but exhibited a wisdom way beyond her years. He was glad of her, but sometimes immensely sad for her.

Ben arrived from the lounge loaded with zest from his micro-sleep. He had a cushion under his arm and was still clutching his Charlie Chalk video.

'Not going Margaret's,' Ben reprised.

'Car,' Gordon said and began ushering him towards the front door. 'Pen. We're going.'

The radio clicked off. Gordon heard Penny locking the back door and switching off the kitchen lights. 'Shall I turn the oven off?' she called, with only the slightest degree of sarcasm.

'Thanks, darling.'

'I want drive,' Ben said, going to the front door of the car and reaching up to tug the handle. Gordon lifted the child and secured him into the harness on the back seat. Pen climbed in and pulled the door shut behind her. Gordon drove away and was half-way down the street before Penny gently reminded him that he had neither closed the front door nor remembered his briefcase.

Miranda had walked through the iron gates of the park. She had twenty minutes to fill before she was due to be picked up and wanted to spend it somewhere she could find some peace. She sat on a bench by the lake and watched a grey city swan drop from its holding pattern in the ruined sky, release its undercarriage and plough to a stop in the lazy current. Corporation debris bobbed by the bank in its wash. The swan taxied threateningly towards her. Miranda stared it out, and it steered away to kerb-crawl a woman with a push-chair.

Miranda unzipped the secret pocket in her handbag and pulled out a crumpled packet of ten Silk Cut, along with a box of matches, a packet of extra strong mints and a breath freshener spray. She lit up the stale cigarette and drew hard until she could feel the tar troubling her throat. She crossed her legs and looked at her knees through the sheer black nylon. She flexed her fingers and examined the back of her hand, then she pinched herself and waited for the flesh to unwrinkle. She was ageing. Late nights were no longer taking hours to get over but days. The next ten years would be the worst, then it would be over and she'd be able to stop pretending to be young.

Miranda brushed her auburn fringe and felt it fall back like the teeth of a comb to its immaculate line. The dress had cost her nearly two hundred pounds. It was by no means in Sandy's league, but nearly a hundred more than she usually paid. It was petrol blue. It had seams that pulled the cloth to her breasts, to her hips, to every place it should be pulled. It matched her eyes perfectly. It was too short. And Gordon hadn't even noticed it. He was too busy tying his bloody stupid tie; the one with the stupid pattern; the one with the stupid pattern that didn't match his stupid jacket or, indeed, any jacket that he had. She wondered if Gordon noticed her at all. Whether he ever fancied her nowadays. Whether he'd be capable of it even if he did. She couldn't remember the last time they'd had sex.

Well, she'd given him enough chances. More than enough. Now it was her turn. There was a date stamp on infidelity. The time to stop indulging in it was the time you could no longer wear your hair long and your dresses short. The time to stop was when your own kids brought their own kids round so that you could remember what it was about them that you loved in the first place. Then you had to grow up. Miranda knew she could still indulge in infidelity with dignity. She wanted affection. She wanted to be wanted.

She stubbed out her cigarette and flicked it towards the swan which had circled back for a second look. The filter bobbed, the swan nosed at it then looked at her with sympathy. Miranda went back to the park gates to wait for her lift. The woman with the crying child in the pushchair watched her enviously, imagining a life for her that they would both have wished for.

Gordon traversed the staffroom and stood pouring lukewarm water from the kettle onto the coffee granules at the bottom of the viral mug. Few of his colleagues could manage anything beyond a sociable grunt or a half smile over the rim of their coffee cups. The spent force had fought hard to reach this peaceable no man's land between the battlefronts of home and classroom; this sanctuary in which the hung-over, despairing, ill-equipped army could rest, attend to the sick and prepare for the next offensive.

Gordon slumped into the posture-damaging seat beside Brian Monnery who was flicking through the appointments pages in the *Times Higher Ed* with the sanguine despair of a man checking his football pools coupon.

'Mm,' Gordon said.

'Fm,' said Monnery.

Gordon unsheathed his *Guardian* from his briefcase, shook the large society section into the wastepaper basket, skimmed the news pages then settled comfortably down with the television review in the tabloid section. He often wondered why he didn't go the whole hog and simply buy a tabloid each day but that, he recognised, would be a sign of defeat.

Anyway, nobody bought the *Mail* or the *Express* other than the Maths department, and only Renton Smear, the sports head, ever bought anything with tits in it.

'Did you see that *Screen* . . . you know, the BBC 1 effort, last night?' Monnery said.

'No. Went out.'

'Piss poor it was. Piss poor. It had whatshername in it . . .'

'Mm?'

'She was in that . . . you know . . . the thing about public school.'

'Oh, her.'

'It was godawful. I slept through most of it.'

'We went to Piran's.'

'Oh yes?' Monnery's attention clocked on. 'And how's Sandy?'

'Sandy is . . .' It was at that point that the dream of what had happened in Sandy's bedroom broke. Gordon blushed brightly.

'Yes?' Monnery fished.

'She's fine.'

'Yes?' Monnery knew he was on to something. He had never met Sandy but, one night, he and Gordon had drunk far more than they intended and what Gordon imagined was going to be a sharing of confidences ended with him offering Monnery the unexpurgated version of his life with Sandy. The gist of it was that Sandy and Gordon had met at university and moved up to London after graduation. Although never explicitly stated, they had both assumed they would, one day, probably, marry. That was until Gordon met Miranda at a summer school and everything went wrong. Or right, depending on whose side you were on. Having offered this to Monnery, Gordon realised his several large pre-dinner gins had given him a head start and that Monnery was not going to offer anything in return. The physicist had made use of the information sparingly but effectively ever since.

'I split some wine. That's all. It was embarrassing. I think I probably made a fool of myself.'

'You're hitting the juice a bit hard at the moment, aren't you?' 'Juice' was a Monnery word. He lived a vicarious life through his wife Jan's extensive collection of second-rate post-war American literature.

'No. No more than . . . well, no more than usual.'

'Miranda thinks you are.'

'Does she? . . . well, she hasn't said . . . I mean, not in as many . . . actually, perhaps she has.'

'Well, she told Jan you were.'

'And Jan told you?'

'Jan tells me everything,' Monnery said smugly.

It always came as a shock to Gordon to realise that he figured in Miranda's thoughts when they were apart. It was a greater shock to learn that he also figured in her conversations. He felt an acute sense of betrayal. Jan Monnery was not the type of person to confide anything to. She brokered confidences with the morality of a stock market trader, which indicated to Gordon that Miranda knew that the conversation would sooner or later get back to him. Perhaps she was genuinely concerned. Perhaps there was a genuine need for concern. No. He could stop drinking tomorrow if he wanted. Easily.

'Fancy a pint at lunch?' Gordon said.

'Are you joking?'

'No. Of course I'm not joking.'

'Can't. Sorry.' As Monnery struggled out of the low chair Gordon realised that his monthly allowance had probably run out. Jan handled the Monnerys' finances with the same iron discipline her mother had exhibited in administering hers. The difference between them, however, was that Jan's mother raised five children on her own whereas she and Brian had a reasonable joint income and only one colourless child of indeterminate sex, Connie. Jan offered Connie for baby-sitting duties and they used her when they couldn't get anybody else. Connie startled Ben with her intensity, and Pen tended to use her appearances as excuses for an early night.

Monnery waddled loathsomely from the room. Gordon skimmed the television section of the paper then folded it neatly into the bin. It had taken him no more than five minutes to read it from cover to cover. There had been a time when global issues actually interested him. He was genuinely fascinated with the break-up of the 'former Soviet Union' as they had taken to calling it. And he was as much of a sucker as anyone else for wars or famine. But nowadays he was so jaded that even graphic descriptions of members of the Royal Family having sex with commoners while being videoed by MI5 barely rated a skimming of the first paragraph. He did, however, always get caught up in child abduction cases. They triggered a deep sense of guilt about the role he was playing in his own children's upbringing, and it was the guilt that propelled him on to read the full coverage. Child murders just made him feel sick for hours.

Renton Smear dropped weightlessly into Monnery's seat and tensed his biceps. His triceps responded accordingly through the thin gauze of his white sports vest. Smear counted to five, then relaxed before doing a series of half sit-ups. His thinning fair hair was already plastered to his temples from the exertion, his square jaw squarer than was humanly possible. Only the small frogspawny pin-prick of his eyes let him down, otherwise Gordon would have found it impossible to have spent any time at all in his company.

'Message for yer. In the office. Chunder was after yer.'

Smear slumped back, panting a little.

'Phone message?'

'Pass.'

'Well does he want me there now?'

'I should think so. Yer.'

'Thanks.'

'Football on the Rec. Sat am. Be there. Staff vs sixth form.'

Gordon accelerated away, pretending not to have heard.

The head's office was rarely visited by any member of his staff. Chunder's authority had slowly waned over the ten years Gordon had been at the school. He had lost his enthusiasm for the place and, having done so, lost the respect of the staff soon afterwards. Chunder was now rarely spotted except at assemblies and speech days. He held no staff meetings and circulated his instructions and wishes direct to the staff via their pigeon holes. Even these slim, stapled missives generally went unopened for days. So it came as no surprise to Gordon to find Chunder's office empty. The room was dominated by a large board bearing the names of each member of staff, each classroom and workshop and each class number. The daily manoeuvres were plotted by a series of coloured pins whose position made no sense to anybody but Chunder. Gordon ran his hand across the prone pins and felt his palms tingle. Chunder's survival lay in his brilliance for creating working systems.

Gordon poked through the loose-leaf mess of sick notes and apologies for absence on Chunder's secretary's desk for any sign of his message. He was about to walk out when he found the large black message book open on a wide shelf by the door. His name was on it, then a colon, then a telephone number and a red spidery star which he took to mean 'urgent'. Gordon didn't immediately recognise the number.

It was not, as he had feared, the telephone number of either Ben's minder or Pen's school, which led him to assume that it must have something to do with Miranda. The notion that immediately sprang to his mind was that she had decided to leave him and that she was phoning to let him know. He then realised how ludicrous this was. Not so much in its general concept but more in its execution. If Miranda had decided to leave he knew she would have told him that morning. Gordon picked up Chunder's phone, poked a number of buttons until he heard a dialling tone, then dialled the number.

'Hello,' the voice said.

'Sandy?'

'You sound surprised.'

'Well of course, I mean . . . yes, I suppose I am.'

'And you're wondering what I want.'

'No. Yes. No, I mean it's nice to hear . . . I mean. Yes, what do you want?'

'I've just given Clive the flick.'

'Yes?' The use of the colloquial catapulted Gordon back to the time when their shared sense of irony was the cement that bound them together. It was he who had first seen it in her: the stand-offish girl dancing much too freely with the spotty lad at the disco. Somehow he had taken the boy's place and somehow they had ended up in her bed.

'I thought you'd be interested.'

'Interested?'

'After last night. I mean I just thought you might have been, that's all.'

'I'm sorry,' Gordon said, mustering sympathy.

'No. I don't want you to be sorry. It's something I should have done ages ago . . . he was making me so . . . so fucking miserable.'

Gordon looked round quickly. Chunder drew the line at

profanity and for a split-second Gordon wondered whether the phone might either be tapped or on a party line. 'Yes. Yes, I could see that.'

'I knew you could. But then you see everything, don't you?'

'Don't be ridic . . .'

'I loved making love to you last night . . . Gordon.'

'Fm? . . . ahherm?' There was a distant click on the line. Gordon pictured an unmarked Transit van in the street outside; two men chain-smoking as they listened in to their conversation. Tape recorders slowly churning, each word recorded for posterity.

'Didn't you?'

'Ah . . .'

'Oh, it doesn't matter. Goodbye, Gordon.'

'No. Don't go.'

'Alright.'

'I mean. I mean, I just don't know what to say.'

'Say one of two things. Say you loved it too or you didn't.'

'Of course I did.'

'Of course,' she mocked. 'Are you happy, Gordon?'

'Yes. No. Well, sometimes. Sometimes I'm happy.'

'No you're not. You're disappointed. Just like the rest of us. But I could make you happy again.'

'How?'

'I think that's up to you to decide.'

'Is it?'

'Yes . . . look. Call me. You've got my number. Perhaps we could meet.'

'For a drink?'

'When?'

'Today?'

'Alright.'

33

And Gordon was hooked. As Sandy chose to see it later, Gordon had been all too ready to take the bait. Gordon, of course, chose to see it quite differently. But somewhere in the dark cavern of Gordon's soul a bell tolled and the companionable slug awoke. At first he raised his blind head with irritation. He was unused to being called upon in the mornings. But as he slithered stickily from his lair he was glad that he had been called.

Gordon sailed through the morning's timetable with little reference to the external circumstances. Having been used to engaging only a small part of his brain in educating his half-witted charges in the Economic History of Industrial Britain he found that he was answering questions purely by reflex. And when the morning break came he was wrongfooted when Monnery retracted his earlier refusal and agreed to accompany him to the pub at lunch.

'Sorry,' Gordon busked, 'Other arrangements.'

'Sandy, then, is it?' Monnery said, floating his usual insinuation.

'What!' For a moment Gordon wondered whether it was Monnery who had been in the Transit van listening in to his conversation.

'Don't get jumpy. I was simply asking if you weren't having a drink with old flamette, Sandy.'

'No. Of course I'm not. I'm having a drink with . . .' Gordon froze and his mind made a split-second inventory of the friends he had that neither Monnery, Jan, nor Miranda could possibly intersect on. The file came up empty. Instead his mind served him the image of a pack of 'Happy Families' cards he had been playing with with Pen the night before. It was a game that neither had wanted to play but both felt better for having spent time together playing. Pen saved him again. 'I'm actually having a drink with Mr Bun . . .' Mr Bun the Baker would have stretched even Monnery's boundless credulity. 'Mr Bunyan.'

'Bunyan?' Monnery tried.

'Yes. He's . . . he's an old lecturer. Retired now of course. But he's passing through on his way to . . . Egypt. Poor old git. I think he's a bit . . .'

'Bonkers?'

'Of course. Anyway, thought I'd do my bit for the old alma mater. Smear took the message.' Gordon leaped gratefully onto the final stepping stone of near truth.

'Smear wrote it down? I find that hard to believe.'

'I think so,' Gordon enjoined happily. 'It was in wax crayon of course, and all in capitals, but he managed somehow to get the message onto a piece of paper.'

'He's trying to muster a team for Saturday. Did he mention it to you?'

'Yes. I'm afraid he did.'

'And are you going?'

'Of course not. I'd rather . . . I don't know what I'd rather do. Impale myself on rusty railings or something. But the thought of running round the Rec with Smear on a day off is just . . .'

'Absolutely. Absolutely. Why waste good drinking time eh?' Monnery punched Gordon playfully on the shoulder and wandered off, laughing heartily in the hope that somebody would ask him what the joke was. The laugh ran out of steam as he rounded the corner of the empty corridor. Gordon spent the rest of the break in the lavatory, faced another hour and three quarters of vacuous questioning, then drove to the Swan to meet Sandy.

Gordon arrived first and got the drinks in which enabled him to shoot a large Scotch down before carrying the pint of 'Best' and gin and slimline to a booth out of sight of the door of the pub. The Swan had been a favourite of theirs when Sandy and he were still a couple, when irony sometimes influenced their choice of places to visit. The furniture was as old and jerry-built as the Victorian building; tall-backed wooden stalls occupied each cranny, and the large filthy windows allowed little natural light to contaminate the atmosphere. There was no jukebox and the food was so bad that at lunchtime the place was almost empty. It was also far enough away from school to minimise the chances of anyone catching them together.

It was the prospect of being caught that set Gordon wondering what he was actually doing there: meeting a woman in a quiet, out-of-the-way pub: a pre-arranged liaison that allowed no interpretation beyond what it actually was – a clandestine meeting of putative lovers.

He knew he would have to work up the story of Bunyan so that not only would Monnery be pacified but he'd also have something to offer Miranda when she asked him what sort of a day he'd had. In fact, he realised, it was quite important to mention it to Miranda because if somehow Monnery mentioned it to Jan and Jan mentioned it to Miranda before he did then she'd surely sense that something was going on. The only other option was to come clean to Miranda and explain that he'd had to invent Bunyan to get rid of Monnery. That, however, was not entirely satisfactory either. Because he could then envisage a situation where he'd have to use Bunyan as a decoy to get rid of Monnery and then, just possibly, have to invent somebody else to explain to Miranda what he was up to. Deceit was exhausting but Gordon decided he'd got it all quite clear in his mind when Sandy slid into the booth beside him and inserted her tongue wetly into his right ear.

THREE

'WHY DID YOU sleep with Miranda?' Sandy said after her second drink. They had spent the first reminiscing about university.

'Do we have to talk about that now?' Gordon said, knowing full well that if they could clear this hurdle then they had a chance of something together. If not, then they must inevitably part – probably with more rancour than they had the first time. How they had remained in contact, friends even, always surprised him.

'Why?' Sandy was studying the blackboard above the bar, but her left hand was clamped to his thigh and he felt her nails cutting through the worn cord of his trousers.

'Because. Because I was drunk . . . because I was young.' He broke off but her face was still determinedly looking away. 'And stupid . . .' he offered. In truth, he would never really know why he had slept with Miranda, beyond the fact that the novelty of somebody actually wanting him to had shocked him into acquiescence.

'You'll have to do better than that. Much better.'

'And . . . because I thought I could get away with it.' Perhaps that was closer to the truth. 'But consequences, well, they were different then. I mean the notion of cause and effect . . . everything seemed possible, didn't it? There was an . . . I don't know, an . . . Sandy, are you alright?'

'No, Gordon. Not really.'

Sandy had never been alright. Being 'alright' was beyond her, just as it was beyond him. *All* of it would never be right. The best they could hope for was that those parts that were right outweighed those that weren't. For a short while, Gordon had been convinced that Piran was capable of filling the gaps in her happiness. He now knew that no single person ever could.

'I'm sorry,' Gordon said, more in despair than apology. He took Sandy's chin in his hand; her face was now cast to the floor so that her long hair had fallen forward to curtain off her expression. A warm tear moistened his thumbnail.

'It just seems such a waste. Fifteen years apart. I feel, I don't know, we could have been together.'

'Would we have lasted?'

'Probably not . . . but I'm glad to see you've not lost the ability to ask the wrong question at the wrong time.'

'I'm sorry. I didn't mean . . .'

'No. I know what you meant. I can read you, Gordon – don't you remember? I know you never actually say what you mean. I also know that like most men you'd do anything for a quiet life – even if that ultimately means hurting people. Don't look at me like that. I know you're weak – and . . . and just so fucking irritating at times. And I sometimes wonder just how much of it is a game.'

'Oh, come on.'

'Don't you ever wonder that?'

'No. It's not a game. I don't play games. I mean, not consciously, anyway.'

'Of course you don't. I would have liked to have had children with you. I miss . . . I mean I envy you Pen . . .

sometimes I imagine she's ours. Sometimes I see myself in her. Stupid isn't it?'

'Of course not.'

'Why did you sleep with Miranda?' Like Poe's pendulum, the accusation returned; swinging lower, cutting through a layer of cloth then another and another until finally it would penetrate his flesh.

'I don't know.'

'You see, I could have fought for you. But I was so hurt that all I could do was fight you. I hated you. I wanted to kill you. That's a measure of how much I loved you.' Sandy looked at him: a bright, brave look that penetrated the film of her tears.

'And do you still hate me?'

'As much as ever.' Sandy leaned against the tall back of the wooden booth. Her hand went to the familiar place at his neck. The barmaid was watching them, absently drying a glass.

Why *did* he sleep with Miranda? He slept with Miranda because he wanted to leave Sandy, and the leaving would never have taken place if something hadn't precipitated it. But he wanted to leave Sandy because he wanted to save himself. And, somehow, he hadn't.

'Why now? I mean, why go through all this now?' It was a question Gordon addressed as much to himself as to Sandy. But there was only one reason for it as far as he could see: what had happened the night before. If it hadn't been for that then they wouldn't have had to confront anything. Now they did.

'I think you know why. And it wasn't just because of last night.' Yes, it was true, Sandy had always been able to read Gordon's mind. Luckily for him, not always this accurately. 'Nor was it because I wanted to get even with Miranda. I quite like her. I like her because I know how important it is to you for me to like her. Why that should bother me I don't know, but it does. We're both alike, she and I . . . What were we . . . ? Yes, the reason we have to go through all this now is because we didn't go through it then. And we should have done. For both of us. Alright?'

'Mm. I suppose so.' Gordon hated 'going through' things. It was something Miranda was always making him do. And the result was usually anger or tears. Sometimes both. Men, at least the men he knew, never seemed to feel the need to 'go through' things. They went through them at the same time as going through them. Women, on the other hand, needed to wait for the sonic boom of meaning before they allowed themselves to lay events to rest.

The problems occurred when the boom was of a different order of magnitude from the one they expected. In the cases where women were exclusively involved, 'going through' things was a stock-taking measure in which motives could be ascribed intentions, slights attached or disentangled from a broader hormonal context depending on whether or not it was necessary for offence to be taken, and compliments filed for times of lean self-esteem. Where both men and women were involved, 'going through' things was simply a blame-laying process.

'Are you all right, Gordon?' Sometimes Sandy wrong-footed him completely by threatening a soul-searching session then knocking him off-balance with a well-placed question.

'Me?'

'Yes, you. I want to know if you're all right. You. Yourself.' She fixed him with a frank stare. 'Really all right.'

'What do you mean "all right?" '

'Content. Fulfilled . . . you know. Alive?'

'Oh, that. Yes, I think I draw breath now and again.' Gordon was glad that the Miranda thing seemed to be out of the way, but they were still dangerously close to mining Sandy's deep vein of misery.

'Don't be glib. You're always glib. Stop pushing me away and talk to me. Here. I'm here.' Sandy tugged his face away from the inactivity of the bar. 'So. Start again. Talk to me.'

'Are we talking about you or me here?'

An executive couple came into the pub, charcoal-suited, wide-shouldered, talking loudly enough to suggest to the sparse clientele that they were trying to hide something. Another illicit couple on another lunchtime liaison. They sensed that the room had sussed them and skulked to a corner table where they took each other's hands and leaned close across their shared bottle of designer water so that their immaculate high-rise haircuts were almost touching.

Sandy watched the couple for signs of discord. 'You always did know how to hurt me.'

'I'm not trying to hurt you.'

'I suppose you think that makes it better.'

'No. I don't think that. You always imagine everything I say has some sort of ulterior meaning.'

'It does. Even though you might not realise it at the time.'

'I have to go.'

'Run away then.'

'I'm sorry.'

'Stop apologising. It's pathetic.'

'I'm sorry, Sandy. I'm truly sorry. This isn't right.' The other couple were kissing now. Tender kisses, flicking tongues that suggested a wider vocabulary of shared passion. Sandy wanted it, Gordon hadn't the strength for it. He felt sick with the sense of betrayal.

'This isn't right? What about last night then?'

'It's the same thing. The same thing.'

'Christ! I'll bet you didn't go through all of this soul

searching when you first fucked *her*. I'll just fucking bet you didn't.'

'It was different. It was a long time . . .'

'And you loved her more than you loved me?'

'I'm sorry.' Gordon leaned down to kiss Sandy solemnly on the cheek but she turned away.

'I'll tell Miranda.'

'What?'

'I'll tell her that we slept together.'

'You wouldn't.'

Less than ten miles away, Miranda was in another bar waiting for a drink. It was a hotel bar, the significance of which was not lost on either her or the man she was with. It wasn't the first time she had been in this hotel bar with this man. But, somehow, it was always necessary for her to pretend that it was. It added to the excitement. Miranda's partner was at the bar chatting to the barmaid who was giving as good as she got. Miranda had made up her mind that if he didn't bring their drinks to the table in the next two minutes then she'd walk out. Contrary to what he seemed to imagine, the setting for their lunchtime drink didn't allow him licence to pursue every other female in the room. The man obviously didn't consider this to be an insult. They were at the hotel. His work was done. It was in the bag. A couple of drinks more and they'd be upstairs in a short-let room passing a passionate afternoon together. But Miranda had already made up her mind; he'd have to work bloody hard to get her across the sordid reception with the sticky carpet, past the priapic porter in the crimson uniform, and into the latticed lift.

The man was back at the table with thirty seconds to spare, but he made the immediate mistake of commenting on the barmaid's legs. Miranda stood up, picked up her handbag and waited for him to move so that she could manoeuvre round the small corner table and leave.

'There are those', the man said, sitting fast, 'who see life as a morality tale. And there are those who don't.'

Miranda sat back down. The barmaid was watching them, or, to be more precise, watching the man.

'Make your choice.' Her partner met the barmaid's gaze and winked. 'If you're not a Catholic it's not necessary to live like one. Alright, love?' They had been discussing faith when he had suggested the drink.

'I suppose you are.' Miranda sipped her gin, sipped it again then downed it and chewed the last bitter traces from the ice cube.

'Of course. But it does have its benefits. A tariff for example. Three Hail Marys for an extracurricular shag . . . a pilgrimage in exceptional circumstances. I wouldn't be without the sacrament.' The man poured out his American beer. The gold liquid chased the white foam up the glass and trapped it at the rim.

'You're so smug.'

'Some wonderful iconography. A sense of theatre . . . unprotected sex . . . you name it we've got it. What do you have?'

'Thrush. Usually.'

'That's just a different sort of guilt. You're burning up inside, Miranda.'

'What did you say to that tart behind the bar?'

'I said I was a priest.'

'And she said?'

'She said . . . I envy you. That's what she said.' The man looked round, another woman had entered the bar. He raped her with a look then pivoted back. 'So, tell me what you want to do. Your choice. I'm not going to push you. I don't want your guilt. Let's not pretend to be some married

43

couple.' You have options. Unlimited options. At least for a few hours.

'There are no such things as unlimited options.'

'Yes there are. But you have to recognise them. Or at least earn them.'

'How? By hurting people?'

'That's one way. Interesting that you see it as your first option. I was thinking more of honesty.'

'Honesty hurts. Sometimes.'

'Not in the long run. Ever.'

Miranda felt the dead weight of the man's hand on her knee. It slid towards the hem of her dress, then stopped and gripped her thigh. 'I could tell you that you should never wear a dress like that. I could say that you were too old for it. That you look like a tart. You'd be hurt but you'd never wear it again. You'd be glad of my honesty in the long run.' His face was close enough to hers for her to smell the beer on his breath, to see the tiny blood vessels broken on his cheeks: a map marking the route from the debauchery of his past to the escalating abuse of his future.

'Take your hand off my leg.' Miranda felt stupid, as she always did with this man. But what annoyed her most was that because his motives were so transparent, she knew she ought to be able to deal with him much more easily. Except it didn't seem to work like that. He gave her nothing to go on. Nothing to untangle except something buried so deep that she couldn't reach it. 'Do you want me to be a tart? I mean, that's what you want me to be, isn't it?'

'I mean. I mean. I mean. What do you mean? What do you want? You. You. You. What is it that you want? Take a while to think about it. I'm not the predator here. Unless that's what you want me to be.'

Miranda kissed him full on the lips. His hand reached

44

higher up her leg and didn't stop when it reached the hem of her dress.

45

FOUR

GORDON WAITED AT the school gates for Pen. A posse of her classmates arrived and she trailed behind them, burdened by two plastic bags and a flute case. She looked like a bearer on a jungle expedition, a Sherpa resigned always to serve and never to lead. Gordon kissed her on the top of her head. She smelt of double maths in airless rooms.

'Good day?' Gordon enquired after they had begun the silent troop towards the car.

'Mm. Alright.'

Gordon knew that when he talked to Pen nowadays it was always he who initiated the conversation. He grasped for something that would evince a response beyond the mild world-weary irritation his clumsy efforts usually provoked.

'I know,' he said. 'Let's do something different.'

'When?' Pen said cautiously.

'Now.'

'Not go home you mean?'

'If you like.'

'What about Mummy?'

'Well, we could take her with us.'

'And Ben?'

'Well . . . we could take him with us.'

46

They had reached the car. Gordon relieved his daughter of her packages and dumped them in the boot. A group of seniors walked by swearing profusely and sharing an un-tipped cigarette. Pen seemed not to notice. At ten, it seemed, profanity was no longer profane enough to warrant a response.

'Let's eat in town,' Gordon said, appalled at the lack of his imagination.

'With Ben?'

'Well . . .'

'He'll spoil it. He always spoils it when we go out.'

'But he's just a . . . well, he's very small still.'

'I know he is but there's no point.'

'Alright. We'll just go back then shall we?'

'Yes.'

Ben lifted the mood in the car. He had, it seemed, hurt himself during the day and he spent much of the journey examining the microscopic cut on his knee. Gordon had no difficulty in communicating with Ben. The child had few needs beyond those that could immediately be satisfied with food, attention, plasters or sleep. They arrived home and Pen went upstairs to change while Ben went into the living room and emerged again with his Charlie Chalk video.

'One video,' Gordon said and posted it into the mouth of the machine. Ben was immediately transfixed by the copyright protection message that flashed onto the screen. The child tugged a cushion up to his chin, sucking the first and second fingers of his right hand up to the knuckle. He sat, small and perfect like a little Buddha, on the settee. Gordon watched the images dancing across his son's eyes and thought of Larkin's phrase; of the 'forgotten boredom' of his childhood. If Larkin had had a video recorder, if his parents had shown him Charlie Chalk videos, would that boredom have been mitigated or compounded?

There was a sharp knock at the front door. Gordon peered round the edge of the curtain. Any visitor between four and six p.m. was to be treated with extreme caution; it was the favourite time for charity callers and unemployed people selling kitchen gadgets. But the glance revealed Piran staring worriedly back down along the street as though he was being pursued. Dusk, or the accumulated pollutants of the day, made the light look grainy and grey.

'Piran,' Gordon said by way of a greeting as he opened the door.

'Shit.' Piran brushed past him, slammed the door and leaned against it breathing heavily.

'Come through.' Gordon steered him into the kitchen, immediately seizing on Piran's arrival as an excuse to pour two generous whiskies.

'Buggering Ada,' Piran rasped.

'Take it easy. Here, drink this.'

Piran managed to gulp the drink down between shallow breaths. It seemed to calm him.

'Now,' Gordon nannied, 'tell me all about it.'

'Bugger. Buggering hell. Give me another one.' Piran thrust his glass towards the whisky bottle. Gordon slugged his own measure down and poured two more.

'So?' Gordon waited until Piran's breathing became easier.

'I'm in for it now, Gordon, and no mistake.'

'Go on.'

'It's such a bloody . . . well, let's put it this way . . . Oh God. God. God. God.'

Pen walked into the kitchen and helped herself to a glass of water. 'Hello, Uncle Piran,' she said to the quivering man leaning against the cooker.

'Hello, Pen.'

Pen looked at her father with an expression he immediately recognised as one from his mother's collection: a superior amusement at those who were unable to plot their lives as efficiently as she was. In a few years' time it would be a weapon she would use against him, but for now he enjoyed the precocity of it. Then she left them.

'Seaman's been arrested. You know, our supplier.' Piran sagged as though a weight had been dropped onto his shoulders.

'Where? I mean why? I mean what happened?'

'He was caught flogging pills at the gates of some school. Idiot.'

'Will that implicate you?'

'Of course it will. He'll take the lot of us down with him, vindictive little turd.'

Gordon closed the kitchen door and steered Piran to the table.

'But I thought you said, I mean you were talking about Mutually Assured Destruction – anyway, they'll need proof, won't they?'

'Yes. Yes, of course they will. But he'll have proof. Of course he'll have proof. I mean he's not stupid, he'll have some insurance against this.'

'Will he?'

'Of course he will. I mean I would.'

'Yes, but then he's not you, is he.'

'Well spotted that man. No, he's not me. But he's clever. I told you he was clever, didn't I? He won't have left anything to chance.' Piran's reputation was founded on second-guessing the motives of the criminal mind. Seaman, as a type, he knew, and he knew well enough to imagine him capable of only the worst.

'Have you spoken to him?'

'Christ no. No.'

'Right.'

'What do you mean "right". I came here for advice. Is that the best you can offer me?'

'You're the legal eagle. I'm not.'

'Yes, I'm sorry. I'm sorry. I'm not thinking straight . . . not thinking at all really.'

'Slow down. Take your time.' Gordon felt like the compère on a television game show.

'I need to find out where he is. Talk to whoever's representing him . . . find out what he's saying.' Piran drew breath and managed a smile. 'I'm sorry. Didn't know where else . . . anyway, I was passing and, well . . .'

Gordon smiled back. Anything more, any acknowledgment of Piran's indebtedness would, he knew, have only made the other man feel worse. But it prompted him to consider just who he would turn to in a crisis. Beyond Miranda, no candidates immediately sprang to mind.

Gordon pointed to the pine shelf beside the freezer. 'Use the phone if you like.'

'Thanks. Yes, thanks.' Piran made two deft phone calls, then helped himself to another drink before making another. Gordon watched him with envy. Having regained his composure, the old Piran was back: brusque, sarcastic, but allowing just enough warmth into his voice to coerce those who were listening gently onto his side.

'Right. Done it. Thanks.' Piran relaxed.

'No problem.'

'It's been a hell of a day . . . sorry if I . . . well, you know. God knows why I came here. Sorry. I mean, didn't want to burden you.'

'That's all right, Piran. Any time. It's no burden. Honestly.'

'Something else. Don't know whether I should tell you.'

'Go on.'

'Probably shouldn't really.' Piran came back to the table, sat down and stretched his legs. 'But, ah, as we're in a laying of the cards onto the table situation.'

'Please. Unburden yourself,' Gordon said, realising as he said it how glib he sounded.

'Sandy's having an affair.'

'Is she?' Gordon swallowed hard.

'Clive called first thing this morning. Said he felt I should know. Smug bastard. Apparently it's been going on for some time. Couldn't tell me who it was . . .' Piran paused, watching the news sink in, trying to judge whether it was, indeed, news to Gordon. Gordon managed to maintain a concerned frown.

'Well. Christ. I mean, Sandy. Christ, who'd have thought . . .'

'. . . So there it is. When I find out who it is I'll hurt him. Have to.' Piran looked up sadly. 'Still. Got to fly. Call you tomorrow. Love to Miranda.'

Piran left, carefully not meeting Gordon's eye. He called a goodbye to Pen through the sitting-room door and Gordon reached the front door just in time to see Piran's black Porsche surge away, back towards the more affluent suburbs. The paperboy watched it enviously as he handed Gordon the weekly free sheet.

Gordon took the paper into the sitting room and dropped it into the wastepaper basket before sitting down beside Ben and attempting to decipher the plot of the video: anything to take his mind from what Piran had just told him. Since that morning, a momentum seemed to have been building; a driving and awful logic had taken hold which Gordon sensed, if he wasn't careful, threatened to destroy everything he had worked for: his home, his life, his marriage, even his children. Ben, seeming to sense this too, and drawn by some strange gravity, fell gently towards him so that his head ended up resting against Gordon's rib-cage. Pen looked up from her homework and smiled maternally. Ben, in a semi-stupor, was a worthy brother. In most other states he was a pain in the neck.

Gordon watched Charlie Chalk through to the end, then went back out to the kitchen to prepare a meal. He was, he realised, in the early stages of shock. More had happened to him in the last twenty-four hours than in the previous ten years. It would be easier, really, to deny it all. To pretend it just hadn't happened.

By the time Miranda arrived home Gordon was past the denial phase and knew he had only one course of action. He had to make a pre-emptive strike to establish his innocence. All that was required was to admit to Miranda that he had had lunch with Sandy, then fill her in on Piran's predicament. All he then had to do was to come up with a reasonable excuse first to Miranda, and then to Piran, as to why he hadn't revealed the lunch date before. 'I know,' he said to Ben, who was perched on the worktop, stirring a vast bowl of pink Angel Delight with a plastic spoon, 'I'll just say that . . . I'll tell her that he just dashed off before I could explain. Which he did of course. Then laugh it off. You see?'

Ben stopped stirring. 'I can't tell you,' he said, which was his stock response to any question.

'No. I suppose you can't,' Gordon said as Miranda came into the kitchen taking off her coat. She looked tired as she went to Ben and kissed him on the head. Gordon drew breath, but before he could embark on his explanation, Ben hijacked Miranda's attention by forcing her to scrutinise the small cut on her knee.

'That's terrible, darling. Terrible.' Miranda used her sympathy as an excuse to gather Ben into her arms and wrap him tightly against her. She kissed him again on the top of his head. He clung to her contentedly like a koala to a tree.

'Good day?' Gordon said as a starter. The moment had passed in which he would simply have been able to launch into his pre-prepared speech.

'Bloody awful.'

'You've laddered your, ah . . .' Gordon gesticulated at the tear that stretched upwards from just above Miranda's right knee to disappear beneath her hem. Miranda ignored the observation and carried Ben from the kitchen, unaware that he was still holding the plastic spoon which was dripping pink Angel Delight onto the back of her dress. Gordon heard a reprise of the opening music to the Charlie Chalk video from the lounge. Pen immediately appeared with her homework, having been displaced from her spot by the fire. Her unzipped pencil case was balanced on top of an open orange exercise book, and she carried it in like a tray of food before dropping it with a telling thud onto the kitchen table.

'All right, Pen?'

'Mm. How do you spell hieroglyphics?'

'Break it down. Hiero-glyphics.'

'H . . .' Pen prompted and Gordon dictated the rest. Then the phone went.

Gordon waited. He was cooking (working), therefore the responsibility for answering the phone lay with Miranda who was watching Charlie Chalk with Ben (a leisure activity). Only when Gordon had been at work all day and Miranda had looked after Ben did the obligations attached to these activities reverse. The phone continued to ring. Gordon turned down the heat under the bolognese sauce and answered it.

'Gordon?' It was Sandy.

'Hello,' Gordon said, over-enthusiastically, but his heart made a cartoon leap into his throat and he felt suddenly nauseous. He knew he had to assess what Sandy wanted before he could divulge to Miranda who was at the other end of the line.

'Piran knows,' Sandy slurred. 'About me and Clive.'

'Ah . . . right,' Gordon said, non-committally. At this point he was using the tone of voice he reserved for time-share salesmen when they called to tell him he had won a twenty-six-inch TV with Teletext.

'I said Piran knows,' Sandy said, inferring from Gordon's tone that he had misunderstood completely what she had just told him.

'Yes. I know.'

'How do you know?'

'Because . . .' Gordon darted a look towards Pen, but she was consumed by her homework. Gordon dropped his voice. 'Because he came round here.'

'He didn't say he had.'

'Well what did he say?'

'He said . . . well, he shouted really, he shouted that he had been informed that I'd been conducting an affair. I mean, he sounded as though he was in court, it was quite bizarre really.'

'Christ.'

'Yes, it's terrible, isn't it? What do I do?'

'Look . . . wait a minute.' Gordon's head was spinning. The heat in the kitchen had begun to close in on him at the same moment as the whisky kicked in. He groped for the wall to prevent himself from falling. 'Look. The thing is that he doesn't know who it is. I mean he doesn't know it's Clive. It was Clive who told him.'

'Clive? Little bastard. I shouldn't have told him about us. I knew it would upset him.'

'What do you mean — about us.'

54

'I told him we were having a thing. That's why I had to break it off.'

'You didn't! No. Sandy. Please.' Gordon felt a slight constriction in his chest.

'Well, I had to tell him something.'

'Look. I can't think about that now. Let's. Let's just sort this other thing ... look, just deny everything. Tell him Clive ... no, don't tell him that, just deny it.'

'I'll try. He's very cross. And pissed. He keeps muttering about semen — I suppose he's gone upstairs to look for evidence.'

'No. No. That's not it at all ... Look, I can't talk now. I'm sorry ...' Gordon was suddenly aware of a hand on his shoulder. Miranda's hand. Miranda's day old perfume approaching from behind. Miranda's face coming round to face him, mouthing 'Who is it?' '... And that's about it, er ... Mr Bunyan.'

'Bunyan?' Miranda mouthed and Sandy voiced in unison.

'Yes. I'll ...'

'I must see you. Tonight. Eight o'clock. Usual pub.' Sandy said, then put the phone down.

'Alright ... yes, I'll speak to Miranda. But it would be lovely to see you before you shoot off to ... em ... Egypt. Okay, bye now.'

'Bunyan?' Miranda said, before he could draw breath.

'Yes, he's ... you know, was, my personal tutor. You remember him. Small; tweed j ... jacket; bald; halitosis.'

'I think that description probably fits the entire faculty, doesn't it?' Miranda helped herself to a glass of Scotch.

'Gammy leg.' Gordon added hopefully. 'I mean one leg. He has one leg.'

'One gammy leg?' Miranda was working hard to place him.

'No. One ... er ... one good leg. The other was ... I don't know, he had gangrene or something. The stench was awful until he had it off. Stinky Bunyan we used to call him. Don't you remember?'

'No. I don't. I think you're making him up.'

'Don't be ridiculous.' Gordon guffawed, knowing he'd gone too far.

'He's going to study hieroglyphics,' Pen said coolly from the kitchen table.

'Is he?' Miranda said, looking sceptically towards her daughter. Gordon was unsure just how much he could get past Miranda's radar – but he knew that his wife and daughter shared an uncanny telepathic communication. Miranda waited for just long enough to see whether Pen would look up and have to meet her eye. But she didn't, so the lie was not tested, and, not having been tested, stood as the truth. Then Ben walked in with his Charlie Chalk video and the tension palpably diminished.

Later, when Miranda was putting Ben to bed, Pen followed Gordon back out into the kitchen and began drying the plates he was stacking on the draining board.

'It doesn't matter,' Pen said.

'Doesn't it?'

'It was only a white lie, wasn't it.'

'Whose. Yours or mine?' Gordon realised he was in his second laying-the-cards-on-the-table situation of the evening, and he was afraid it wouldn't be the last.

'Both. They were both white lies.'

'You musn't lie to Mummy.'

'Alright. Shall I tell her the truth?'

'You should do what you think is right.'

'I do.' Pen dropped her tea towel to the floor, then Gordon felt her hands go suddenly around his waist. 'Don't die, Daddy,' she sobbed.

Gordon soothed the child but he respected his daughter's telepathy and felt a shiver pass down his back. Pen finally broke away and dried her eyes with the tea towel. She didn't apologise for her tears and Gordon was glad of that. For all of his failings as a parent he was glad to have fathered a child who never apologised and rarely explained. He had, he knew, lived too much of his life in abject apology. Sometimes he wondered if all of his life was not an apology, though to whom he could not quite decide.

When Ben was in bed, Gordon went into his dark, warm room and kissed the child on the cheek. Ben reached up and pulled his face close. Gordon allowed the contact, believing it to be the beginning of a game which Ben had devised to delay sleep. But within twenty seconds he realised that the child had fallen asleep and had clamped their faces together for comfort. Gordon pulled Ben's unresisting arm away and folded it beneath the warm cover. He looked at the face, free of all tension, and allowed himself another moment of gratitude. He kissed Ben again then pulled the door to, leaving it sufficiently open to allow a little of the hallway light in.

Downstairs, Pen was watching *EastEnders* with Miranda. Gordon knew that, again, it would be impossible to embark on his prepared speech. He couldn't bear to lie in front of Pen; any further complicity between them would be far too disloyal. Instead, he decided to go and wash before meeting Sandy. Then, having met her, he would sort out the misunderstandings, possibly call round at Piran's to clear things with him then come back and explain it all to Miranda when Pen was in bed and everything was square. Gordon muttered something about going to get ready and went upstairs, changed and washed his face. When he came back down again, Miranda was asleep on the sofa with her legs tucked beneath her and Pen was watching *The Bill*. That meant it was past eight and Gordon was already late.

FIVE

GORDON FOUND SANDY where he had left her some seven hours before. But it was immediately clear that something had happened since their last conversation. Her coat was buttoned tight to the neck; she was nursing a glass of mineral water and staring at her watch as he came across and kissed her on the cheek.

'Piran's gone,' she said, brushing off the contact.

'Gone?' Gordon slid onto the booth beside her.

'Yes. I don't think he wanted to go, but this rather unpleasant little man came round just after I phoned. He answered the door, and the next I knew he was being bundled into a big white car and driven off.'

'Bundled. How?'

'What do you mean "how?" – he was bundled . . . just bundled. Like a parcel.'

'A large parcel?'

'What?'

'Like a large parcel?'

'Are you taking the piss out of me, Gordon? Because, believe me, now is not the time.'

'No. No, of course I'm not.'

'Well what the hell are you getting at? I mean he was

bundled into the car by two men, like a . . . yes, like a large parcel.'

'I was just wondering. I mean, I was trying to work out whether he was being bundled against his wishes. That's all. I mean a large parcel . . . two men bundling a large parcel would imply there was some kind of resistance, whereas a small . . .'

'Why didn't you just ask if he was struggling?'

'Well . . .'

'Yes. He seemed to be struggling . . . a bit, anyway. I mean I suppose they could have just been helping him in.'

'Mm. Same again?' Gordon pointed towards Sandy's glass.

'No, Gordon. And I don't think you should either. I need you sober enough to help me to find Piran.'

'I'm sure he's fine. I imagine he's gone off with Seaman . . . or possibly even the police.'

Gordon went to the bar to fetch the drinks. When he returned he filled Sandy in with the details of his earlier conversation with Piran. It was clear from her reaction that, although she was aware of his cocaine habit, she was unaware of his connection with Seaman, and Gordon's explanation did little to assuage her anxiety over what she insisted on labelling as his kidnap.

'You hear about these drug barons,' she said, 'but I never imagined Piran would get mixed up with them. His brother I could believe. But not him.'

'I'm sure he can look after himself,' Gordon insisted. 'He knows these people, he mixes with them, he knows how their devious criminal minds work – and that's just the police,' he said with questionable timing. 'Now come on – let's talk about something else.'

'Oh, I see,' Sandy said sharply.

'What?'

'You don't give a damn about him, do you? All you're

interested in is yourself and preserving your bloody relationship.'

'That's not fair.'

'Who said anything about fair, Gordon? I don't think you've been entirely fair with me. And unless you help me find out what's happened to Piran, don't count on me to go along with your pathetic lie about what we were up to this lunchtime. Let alone last night.'

Gordon followed Sandy back to the house. The lights of the evening traffic blurred then sharpened between the sweeps of his windscreen wipers. The day was over, the night had not yet begun. Those people still on the streets hurried home as if they were trying to beat a curfew. Gordon found his concentration slipping. Somehow an hour had passed, an hour he couldn't account for, an hour which would need explanation when he returned home. He would have to fill it with details of Bunyan's travel plans, perhaps flesh it out with a little human interest — his late-but-tragic marriage to a German heiress, his archaeological detective work which had led him to his latest discovery . . . Sandy's hazard lights were flashing a warning through the drizzle. They had turned into her street, a well-spaced collection of large white Victorian mansions. A saloon car was parked at the kerb. Gordon slowed and stopped as Sandy drew up. He waited for her to get out then followed her to the house.

'It's the car,' Sandy whispered unnecessarily, pointing towards the saloon.

'Yes. I thought so.' Gordon took her arm and steered her directly up the chequer-tiled path to the front door. There seemed little point in exercising caution. If the house was full of gun-toting drug barons then they'd just have to face the consequences, but Gordon remained convinced that Piran had simply been given a lift to where Seaman was being held by a couple of his acquaintances in the CID.

Before Sandy could slide her key into the lock, the door was opened by Piran. 'Oh. Gordon. I was just . . .' He gestured towards the street. 'Never mind. Come in.'

'I thought I'd, ah . . . come and see, you know. How you are. Just bumped into Sandy on the drive.'

'Mm. Come through.' Piran was distracted. Gordon followed Sandy into the living room. Piran snapped on the large overhead light, robbing the room of its comforting shadows. 'Sit down. Both of you.' He gestured towards the wide sofa. Sandy flashed Gordon a warning look.

'No. Look . . . I'll . . .' Gordon hovered, half-sitting. 'Now I know you're alright, I'll shoot off. Give you two a . . .'

'You must have had a laugh this evening, Gordon.' Piran said. 'A huge laugh at my expense.' Piran's indecision was gone. His distraction had been a mask for his rage. Gordon had the good sense to say nothing. 'I mean all of that sympathy. Simply oozing out of you. Christ, Gordon. I believed you. I believed in you. We all did . . . and then you go and screw my wife.'

'Piran,' Gordon tried. 'I know what you're think . . .'

'No. Don't even try to explain. I've heard excuses from the best of them.'

'Piran,' Sandy said.

'Please don't.'

Sandy settled sullenly back into the comfort of the sofa.

'For your information, I called round at Clive's on my way back from bailing Seaman . . .' And Gordon laughed. Despite himself, Gordon laughed. Sandy punched him on the side of his leg, but he was no longer listening. Piran was building up to a full and impressive rage: red-faced, roaring, recriminatory, dredging up past indiscretions, weaving in faux pas. It went on and on but Gordon was gone: away. His mind flew free from the dreadful scene and alighted in a classroom where he saw himself scrawling a chalk date onto the blackboard. The faces before him were blank; actively uninterested. The harder he pressed, the more uninterested they became. Then he was in the staffroom beside Monnery, listening blankly to him telling a long and turgid tale about something he and Jan had done at the weekend. He flew home and found Miranda sleeping, saw himself lying stock still, staring into the dark, all hope of sleep gone. He hovered to Pen's room, watched her sleep, wanting her to wake so that he could say goodbye. Because suddenly, with absolute clarity, he knew he had no choice but to leave. The deceit of others was bearable – just. The deceit of himself was not.

Pen had known for a long time, perhaps Miranda had known, he imagined even Sandy had known, she had certainly made it more inevitable. Why fight to hold it all together when they had for such a long time been apart?

He knew that leaving Pen would be the hardest part. And when it came to it, leaving Pen was the hardest part. She woke and came in to his bedroom to find him packing. Seeing the bruise on his face she slumped onto the bed and began to cry. When he tried to leave she sprang up and held on and wouldn't let him go. For the first time in his life Gordon had to push her away. Miranda's mute hatred was more bearable than Pen's despair. Gordon didn't allow himself to cry until he got out of the house. Then he couldn't stop.

PART TWO

PART TWO

ONE

O F THE FOUR separate conversations being conducted at the table, Piran and Sandy's was the most intense. Their heads were tented together, their gazes not quite meeting but bisecting at a point just above the centre of the table. Miranda, sitting across from them, was continuing a formal and rather dull conversation with a tall, rangy man called Stephen. He was one of Piran's old school friends who worked in a bookshop. From the way he dressed, he looked like a penurious poet but he carried himself with the casual agility of a sportsman.

Of the remaining four, Clive and Anne were the most animated, but Anne's most intimate pronouncements had always been made publicly, while the quiet woman and her husband seemed content to bat occasional observations between each other tightly wadded with meaning. Anne had earlier suggested to Miranda that she thought the quiet couple were stoned and Miranda, who was the only sober one at the table, had agreed with her assessment.

'I'd like to propose a toast,' Piran said quietly.

'Here we go,' Anne whispered. The others fell silent as Piran raised his glass to head height, looked at it for inspiration then, after a careful pause, said, 'To Sandy.' A ragged chorus echoed Sandy's name. '. . . And to a new life.'

'And to a new . . . ah . . .' Stephen embarked alone, then stopped and blushed. The others knew Piran well enough to know when he was singing a solo. Stephen aspirated a dry laugh but Miranda didn't help him out by joining in.

'Christ,' Anne said, this time more audibly as Piran turned away and resumed his conversation with Sandy. 'I think I'm going to puke. Hasn't he become pompous?'

'What?' Miranda wasn't really listening to any of the conversations, she was concentrating her attention on Sandy who was glowing, or blushing. Either way, she was one of the small proportion of women who could be said to blossom when pregnant. She looked so wholesome that Miranda found it almost impossible to hate her. And she wanted to hate her. She didn't want to be reasonable. It was three months since Gordon had left and, having missed the initial impetus to behave badly, she was looking for a second chance to vent her self-righteous anger. This was the first invitation of Sandy's she had accepted, and then only because Anne had talked her in to it. Having been provided with the dim beacon of Stephen to illuminate her evening added insult to injury.

'. . . Clive said that they found the old man in the bedroom with a porn mag . . .' Anne gatecrashed her attention again, '. . . and, well, one can imagine the rest. What a way to go. He'd been dead for a week, though what he was doing in a bed-sit in Camden is a little hard to fathom . . .'

'Mm?' Clive leaned in to break into the intimacy.

'I was telling Miranda about Piran's father. About the unusual, you know . . .'

'Are we going to play a game?' Clive whispered, 'I'm bored.'

'I'm trying to talk to Miranda, Clive, please don't interrupt unless you have something to add to the conversation.'

'Did he get the house?' Miranda said. Since Gordon had left, money had been tight. She had borrowed from her mother but it was beginning to seem as though she might have to sell the house. She couldn't bear the tension in her mother's voice. It strained for sympathy while all the time Miranda could hear the harmonic 'I told you so'. She believed that she loved her mother, but, increasingly, only in the abstract. The flesh and blood version was becoming harder to bear each time they spoke.

'We play this game,' Clive chortled to Stephen. 'Pick a pop star, writer, doesn't matter what, then describe him – or her – by a brief job description . . .'

'No. His mother's still there.' Anne pushed Clive back into his chair using the table edge to lever her forearm against his breastbone. 'And the brother: Desmond. I suppose it's only a matter of time before he gets it all . . . or at least a good share of it . . . There was some talk of us all going down there for Christmas. You should come, it would give you . . .'

'I'll give you an example: someone who weighs fat women. People. Someone who weighs fat people . . . It's a rock and roll star.'

Stephen furrowed his brow.

'Give up?' Clive said.

'Chubby Checker,' the quiet woman said quietly.

'Yes,' Clive said, losing spirit. 'I didn't think you'd get that one. Your turn.'

The conversation rumbled away like distant gunfire; Miranda tuned out of it again. She couldn't take her eyes from Sandy who was being stifled by Piran's attention. Since the episode with Gordon, Piran had taken the guilt entirely

on himself and decided that his inattentiveness had precipitated her affair. He was more than making up for it now.

'. . . something along those lines.' Anne raised her voice a
notch and Miranda was forced to turn her way again. 'It's
rather like he's become one of those born-again Christians,
isn't it? All squeaky clean and earnest . . .'

'. . . and he says,' Clive interjected, 'the bloke, I'm a
country member. And the doorman says, yes, I remember
. . . see?'

Miranda switched the conversation off. She had not come
for this. 'How long is it now?' she shot across the table
towards Sandy, but the jarring tone she found herself using
was unfamiliar, even to her. Miranda cleared her throat in an
effort to explain, if not to apologise for it.

'I'm sorry?' Sandy had been waiting for this. She pushed
Piran away a little, fanned her face with her right hand and
took a deep breath.

'The baby. When is it due?'

'Oh, let me . . .' Sandy began counting on her fingers.

'Twenty-six weeks,' Piran announced formally. He took
Sandy's hand and clasped it tight.

'You look very well on it.'

'Thanks. I feel, you know, a bit green around the gills
sometimes . . .'

'Twenty-six weeks,' Miranda reflected. 'So it could be
Gordon's then . . . couldn't it?'

Anne immediately lit up a cigarette. The quiet woman
looked at Piran while her husband, a connoisseur of guilt,
focused on Sandy. In the sudden silence Clive was caught
humming a Phil Collins song and tapping out the rhythm
with his fork. Miranda's partner drained his glass.

Sandy sighed hard, centred her attention on the table then
summoned up her strength and, with Piran's help, pushed
her chair back from the table. She walked straight-backed

and with pregnant dignity from the room. Piran waited for her to leave then stared at Miranda, challenging her to say more.

'Well it could. Couldn't it?' Miranda's cool nearly carried it off.

'We made a decision, Miranda. To have a child. We spent a month in the Caribbean, and when we came back, Sandy was pregnant.' In his experience of the courts, Piran had often found that an exposition could be mistaken by a dull mind for an explanation.

'Then it may be black, I suppose.'

Anne translated her shocked laugh into a smoky cough which rumbled for a while like an engine turning over but failing to catch.

'I'm sorry you feel so bitter towards her.'

'But not surprised, I hope.' Miranda had just discovered that she felt just as much bitterness towards Piran. After all, if he'd been a better man then Sandy wouldn't have felt the need to steal Gordon.

'Time to go, children, I think.' The quiet woman stood, and pulled her husband to his feet. Miranda momentarily caught his eye. He held her look. 'A lovely meal, Piran. Will you thank Sandy for us . . . I wonder if you'd like to share a cab?'

'Mm?' Anne said. 'Oh, yes.' Taking the hint she stubbed out her cigarette. Clive frantically downed his wine, then his brandy. As they let themselves out, he touched Piran on the shoulder. Anne's stubbly kiss grazed his face; her goodbyes always lingered abrasively. Piran didn't bother standing. Neither Anne nor Clive had looked at Miranda. Then Stephen stood up, checked his flies and managed to leave the room with a series of semaphored gestures but without actually saying anything. For a moment, seeing that her date had left his bicycle clips on his place mat, Miranda wondered

69

whether he'd just gone to the toilet. The front door slammed, answering the question.

'He's left his clips,' Miranda said.

'I'll take them in on Monday.'

'I hope he doesn't fall off and break his neck.'

'I'm sure he won't.'

'I'm sorry,' Miranda said.

'No you're not.'

'I'm sorry I spoilt the meal then. I'll go up and apologise.'

'Leave her. She'll probably be asleep.'

'Christ, you just don't see it, do you? Or is it that you see and you pretend you haven't?'

Piran changed chairs, taking the one directly across the table from Miranda. He topped up his glass then leaned over and filled hers. 'How's Pen?' With every conceivable right to be angry, he was exacting his revenge by remaining reasonable.

'. . . Oh, you know . . .' Miranda willed Piran's anger to break. Until it did she had nothing on which to strike a spark to ignite her own.

'Look . . .' Piran leaned across the table and took Miranda's hand which had involuntarily clenched to a fist round her knotted napkin. She released it and her anger began to thaw.

'Don't say you know how I feel. Please don't say it.'

'I wouldn't dream of it. I barely know how I feel. From one moment to the next . . . from each day to the . . . sometimes I think I'm going mad with it all. Tell me how Pen is. Allow me some godfatherly concern.'

'It would help if he called. Have you heard from him? I don't suppose, no, he wouldn't, not here, would he?'

'No, he hasn't. Not me, anyway.'

'Pen thinks he's gone to Egypt – with some old professor. He writes her letters about hieroglyphics and the pyramids,

70

but they're postmarked somewhere in the Midlands. I put them in an airmail envelope . . . Oh, I know she knows, but we go along with it for . . . it's ludicrous. I suppose he thinks he's finding himself or something. I just hope he finds himself before I do otherwise I'll kill him.'

'I'm glad you came tonight. I'm glad we can talk about it like adults.'

'I'm not. Not at all . . . she's been, well little girls can be such bitches can't they, she's been completely ostracised by her so-called friends. It breaks my heart. Breaks my heart.'

'Would it help if I called round to see her?'

'Yes, I imagine it would solve everything for her. She'd stop crying in her sleep, find a new set of . . . Oh, God,' Miranda massaged her brow with a tightly knuckled hand. 'Look, yes, why don't you come round. I'm sure she'd like to see you. Do you hate Gordon?'

'Hate him? Ahm, no. No I don't think I quite hate him. I think I feel let down by him. But I really don't suppose I hate him. Do you?'

'No. Not now.'

'No.'

'. . . I wouldn't ever say this to him but, in a strange way, I always knew. No, not knew. I sort of half-expected this to happen. If I hate him it's because . . .'

'Why?' Piran said. 'Why did you, how did you know it was going to happen?'

'No, I didn't . . . I mean, not consciously, not in the sense that I knew it consciously. But he's always been detached. From all of us. But what I was saying was, if I hate him it's because of what he's done to Pen. Not me or Ben, but Pen. I'll never forgive him for that.'

'Will she? Forgive him, I mean.'

'If he comes back, yes. If he doesn't, no. At the moment she blames me. Partly, anyway.'

'Sandy?' Piran let go of Miranda's hand then looked over his shoulder as if he'd heard somebody come into the room, Miranda hadn't heard anything.

Sandy edged guiltily in. 'I wasn't listening.'

'We were talking about Gordon,' Piran conspired.

'Have you heard from him?' From her tone it seemed she had already forgiven Miranda.

'No. I was just telling Piran, he's written to Pen a few times. But we haven't . . .' Miranda bit her lip to prevent herself from crying.

'Is it awful?' Sandy said.

'Yes. It's . . . awful. Awful. The uncertainty. I don't know what he's doing, or where he is, or whether he intends to come back. I can't make any plans.'

'At least none that involve him, I suppose,' Sandy said.

'No, you're right. None that involve him.'

Connie Monnery was vomiting into the kitchen sink. Pen was watching from the door as her baby-sitter's sharp shoulder-blades reached towards each other beneath her thin white T-shirt before tearing apart like a wishbone snapping. Her black jeans hung loose as though she'd bought a pair two sizes too big. Connie had her father's short bull neck and her mother's fine fair hair. She had a certain pride but it was a pride less in her appearance than in denying her abject plainness. She had raided the fridge, eaten the entire contents of the biscuit barrel, choked down half of a raw cabbage and only faltered when she'd started on a pair of raw lamb chops. When the vomiting and the aftershocks of dry heaves stopped Pen passed her a clean tea towel. Connie covered her face with it like a tennis player resting after a hard set. When she put it down, her eyes were moist.

'I didn't know you were up,' Connie said lazily. Connie had always been a lethargic child but, with adolescence, her lethargy had taken a more profound hold on her character. Her father knew, because he had seen it in a hundred of his charges, that if she didn't snap out of it soon there was a danger of it taking root and becoming a philosophy. As usual, when the Monnerys' daughter had arrived to baby-sit, Pen had gone immediately to bed and locked her door. She was half-way through re-reading the latest letter from her father when she had heard Connie puking in the kitchen.

'Shall I phone Mum?' Pen was unconcerned for Connie, she felt nothing for her. If anything, Pen was intrigued by her discomfort. It suggested something demonic and adult. She felt she might learn something from it. 'The number's here. I don't mind calling.' She slid the slip of paper from behind the magnetic letter that was holding it to the fridge door.

'What for?'

'Because you're ill.'

'I'm not ill.'

'Oh.'

'I thought you were asleep.' Connie turned sideways and looked at her reflection in the kitchen window. Her haunted eyes hunted for traces of fat. She was no longer just thin, she was becoming emaciated.

'No. I was . . . I was reading.'

Connie turned on the hot tap and squeezed washing-up liquid into sink. She swished the water round with her hand then pushed some of the more stubborn debris down the small triangles of the plughole with her finger. When she had satisfied herself that the sink was clean she put the washing bowl back in and hung the tea towel over the rail beside the fridge. 'If you tell your mother I'll tell her I caught you smoking.'

'I won't.'

'You'd better not. Come into the lounge.'

73

Pen trailed Connie out of the kitchen then sat obediently beside her on the settee. Connie had been watching the television with the sound turned down. The floor was littered with empty crisp wrappers. 'What do you want to watch?' Connie aimed the remote and flicked through the channels.

'Don't mind.'

The set, re-tuned to its Saturday night hospital soap, flickered mutely. Both girls continued to watch as they talked. As children of the cartoon age, the dialogue was redundant to them.

'Do you watch this?' Connie said.

'Sometimes.'

On the screen a doctor walked into a curtained hospital cubicle. An old woman was lying on a trolley with her handbag clasped to her chest. With one look between the tall doctor and the nurse the girls knew that not only was the woman going to die but also that the doctor and the nurse were having an affair.

'Do you like him?' Connie said.

'He's alright.'

'Who do you like?'

'Nobody, really. Who do you like?'

'Do you know Darren Twigg? He's in year ten.'

'I don't think so.'

'He's my boyfriend.'

'Oh.'

'I'm meeting him after your mother gets back.'

'Do you like my new laces?' Pen pulled her heavy boots from beneath the sofa. The bootlaces were fluorescent yellow.

'Yes. Has your mother got any drink in the house?'

'She's got some gin I think. In the kitchen.'

Connie went out, leaving Pen to watch the old lady die.

Her heart had stopped in the previous scene and they had wheeled her along a corridor to the crash team, signalling the imminent conclusion of the programme. The tall doctor administered metal pads to the woman's chest, everybody stood away, he pressed something and the woman jolted into the air. There was a glimpse of her grey slip. The green graph line on the monitor remained resolutely flat. The tall doctor shook his head, thanked everybody and glanced at his watch. Births and deaths were now timed to the second. Somewhere in the hospital, the administrators were recomputing the three score years and ten to four decimal points.

Connie came back in with a tumbler of gin. 'Did he kiss her?'

'No. She died.'

'No, the doctor. Did he kiss the nurse?'

'Not yet.'

They watched until the closing credits. The tall doctor was marvellously sensitive with the old woman's son who, on hearing of his mother's death, crumpled to a heap on the floor and began sucking his thumb. Two policemen arrived and took him away. The doctor shook his head gravely and managed, in that single gesture, to make many compassionate statements. Pen and Connie were in no doubt that he was in for a hell of a bender when he got home. The nurse, seeing all this, left him without saying a word and the credits rolled.

'Are you sad about your father?' Connie said.

'He's coming back soon. He's in Egypt.'

'I wish my father'd go to Egypt. I hate him.'

'Is that gin?'

'Yes.'

'Can I have a sip?'

'You won't like it.'

Pen took the glass, stuck her finger in, sniffed it, licked it, then sipped the bitter liquid. She didn't like it but it made her stomach feel warm and she had felt so cold and empty since her father's departure that she took another sip.

'That's enough,' Connie said. 'Do you want to watch a video?'

'Alright.' Pen relaxed a little. She had expected to be sent back up to bed so that Connie could continue looking through her mother's drawers and cupboards which is what she always did when she baby-sat. Once Pen had caught her taking some money from a brown envelope, but she didn't tell her mother because, on the rare occasions she felt anything for Connie, she felt sorry for her. Particularly about her father. Connie's father was always trying to make jokes but they weren't ever funny. After her own father had left, he'd come round one night to see if her mother had any jobs she wanted him to do. She told him she hadn't but offered him a cup of coffee. To avoid any more of his jokes, Pen had gone out to the lounge with Ben when she heard her mother shout and then the sound of someone being slapped. Connie's father had rushed past and out of the house and her mother had stayed in the kitchen for an hour and drunk almost a whole bottle of gin. Pen had put Ben to bed, and read him a story. She didn't mind looking after him. But now there was nobody to look after her.

Connie fed the video into the machine and fast forwarded it to a scene in which a tanned supermodel in a brief swim-suit encouraged them to start stretching. She was standing in front of a huge photograph of a palm-treed beach. Connie jumped up and followed the instructions. Soon, too soon, she was panting with the exertion and fell back onto the settee.

'My father fancies your mother,' Connie said.

'I know.'

'How do you know?'

'I can tell.' Pen was becoming more adept at lying.

76

'My parents are always arguing. I think it would be better if they split up. I wouldn't mind. I'd live with my mother. She doesn't care about me going out late. My father's very boring about it. I'm supposed to be back by midnight at weekends and ten in the week. Do you think she's beautiful?'

Pen appraised the model. 'No. I don't like her hair.'

'I think she's beautiful.' She used the word with awe. 'When I leave school I'm going to go to California and work for a fashion agency.'

'That's good.' From Connie's tone, it seemed that the arrangements were already in place.

'I'll probably work with her.'

'I'm going to be an air stewardess. Or a doctor. Or a vet.'

'I think we'd get on. I think she seems a nice sort of person. What will you do if your father doesn't come back?'

'He will.'

'My father thinks he's gone off with a young floozie.'

'What?'

'With a . . .' Having finally prompted a response from Pen she was now sorry. Connie's essential decency would ultimately save her. She would leave home and never see her parents again. 'I don't think he really knows.'

But it was too late. Pen was wounded. 'I don't think he should say things like that.'

Pen went upstairs and locked her bedroom door. She had never considered the fact that her father might actually have gone off with anyone. Other women never figured in her relationship with him, except, of course, her mother. She sat on the bed and pulled out his letters from the bottom drawer of her desk. There were six of them; two for each month he had been away. They described the long journey he was taking with Mr Bunyan through Egypt in search of hieroglyphics (which he always spelt out in capitals). Pen was plotting his progress on a map. He was travelling up the centre of the country and heading for Cairo. Pen was convinced that when he reached Cairo he'd fly home. Her father had never actually said this but Pen knew. She just knew.

'What did you think?' Anne was undressing in front of the mirror. Clive was in bed and had been nearly asleep when his interest was aroused by Anne's black suspenders which she was now stripped down to.

'About what?'

'About Miranda.'

'I thought she looked alright.'

Anne was momentarily naked. Then, with a balletic swirl of heavy fabric, she was installed in the tepee of her thick nightdress and applying cream to her face. Clive's interest immediately waned. 'I thought she looked terrible. I thought it was appalling. Quite appalling. I shouldn't have talked her into going. Stephen was as dull as ditchwatcher.'

'Was he? I liked him. Good bloke. Bit toffee-nosed.'

'Self-obsessed, then. It felt like dullness. Poor Miranda. I wonder whether Sandy did it on purpose.'

'She wouldn't have gone unless she'd wanted to.'

'Did you speak to anybody?'

'I had a word with Piran.'

'And?'

'We're having a beer on Wednesday.'

'Is that all?' Anne hovered at the foot of the bed. It was a habit that always irritated Clive. Unless sex was on the agenda or there was something titillating on the television he could rarely find any reason not to go straight to sleep after a night out.

'Mm. Night.' Clive drifted off. Anne sat on the bed and looked at him. He was sweating slightly from the drink but

78

his face was unlined. She could see why women found him attractive, but she'd never been that attracted to Clive herself. It was the value added to him by the attentions of the other women that prompted her to accept his offer of marriage. He was, in her mother's words, 'unrefined'. She'd hoped that she could change him, but after ten years she realised that she couldn't. As they got older it was clear that the relationship they had was more that of a mother and a son than husband and wife. But that seemed to be no worse than living as brother and sister, which was what she considered many of her other married friends to be.

Clive was not a man who had cares, or could be made to carry cares that weren't his own. And she had tried; the occasional humiliation was all she could manage, but nothing ever lasted. They had nothing to tie them together: neither children, nor secrets, nor a mutual dislike of people, not even shared childhood horrors. He was too balanced and she wasn't unbalanced enough to tip him from his equilibrium.

Anne burrowed irritably under the duvet, tugging her share roughly from beneath Clive who moaned, rolled away from her and reclaimed it. Having pulled it back, she reached to turn out the bedside light. Then the phone rang. Anne's immediate reaction was to look at her watch. It was twelve thirty-seven. Night calls spelt tragedy – or wrong numbers. Or obscene callers. She nudged Clive. He groaned but didn't wake. She pushed him harder. He rolled over, taking the duvet again. Anne lifted the receiver.

'Yes?' It was best to be curt and businesslike. In her book, victims asked to be victims. The line remained silent, then she heard a police siren. It seemed to pass quickly, echoing briefly from the surrounding buildings. She processed the sound. The caller was in a small town; a country town. Surely no city would be that silent at twelve thirty . . . eight. The red numerals of the alarm swapped places. Anne gathered the flex of the phone in her right hand. She wanted the caller to stay on the line. It was immaterial whether he wanted to talk. She just wanted him to stay on. It was a him. That she also knew. Instinctively. 'Hello . . .' she whispered. Perhaps he was a victim. Perhaps he wanted to be treated like a victim. She heard breathing. Laboured.

'Am . . .' Yes, it was a him: 'am?', 'em?' She waited for him to continue. 'Ahm . . . tell her I'm sorry.'

'Gordon?' Anne said to the dialling tone.

TWO

'Are you sure it was Gordon?' Miranda had been awake for much of the night, as had Anne who had initiated the call. They were standing in their respective kitchens, striking identical poses at similar work surfaces. Their tables were laden with breakfast cereals, chosen for their weight-reducing, bowel-cancer-arresting properties rather than any considerations of nutrition or taste. Mortality was top of the menu at the breakfast table. By 'supper', the day having taken its toll, the fats and toxins would be welcomed back for comfort and release. On their radios the ritualised pedantry of the *Today* programme was reassuring them that their respective worlds had woken safely. Disaster had tidily confined itself to the usual continents. Two hundred had died, and one Briton was believed to be missing. The storm which had raged all night was still strafing the overgrown lawn with sharp tracers of rain. A white tea towel hung limply on Miranda's washing line like a flag of surrender.

'I'm almost sure.' Anne was careful. She knew what she was dealing with and, for once, she was just trying to impart information rather than trade it, doctor it, or augment it.

'Almost? Well, what did he say?' A death would have

disturbed Miranda no more profoundly. Her anxiety soared to a critical level.

'He said, "Tell her I'm sorry", that's all. I did try . . .'

'Well why didn't he call me?'

'I really . . .'

'I mean if he has something to say you'd think the least he could do was to say it to me. Jesus Christ, I mean . . . that's typical of Gordon. Absolutely fucking typical.'

Pen came in to the kitchen. From the landing she had heard her father's name. Her small flurry of hope died when she saw her mother's face. She looked as if she was going to cry. Pen went to the table and poured Ben's cereal into a plastic bowl. Then she poured out her own, soaked it in milk, and began the joyless consumption of the milk-sodden lumps of wheat. The first mouthful always made her feel sick. Milk, however fresh, always tasted sour. Cereals were boring. She had woken with the belief that she would never see her father again. Life could only be described by the words she was not allowed to say.

'I'm sorry, Anne. I just think you should have . . . I mean either you have something to tell me or you don't. It's typical of you that you use something like this just to wind me up. Don't you understand! Don't you understand what we're going through? Doesn't anybody have the least idea! Jesus.' Miranda slapped the receiver onto its cradle then stood looking at it, trying to get a hold on her exhaustion and anger before she joined Pen at the table.

'It doesn't matter,' Pen said, feeling she was being called on to say something.

'She makes me so . . . cross.' Miranda clicked on the kettle switch, at the same time lifting the kettle and shaking it, even though she had filled it with water just before the phone rang. And she knew she had filled it with water before the phone rang. It was just another habit, and if her rituals were becoming so obvious to her, God knows what they must seem like to Pen. Without Gordon, she was scrutinising herself more closely. She was afraid she was searching for the reasons for his desertion in her own behaviour. It was tiring and destructive but she just couldn't stop herself.

The phone rang. Pen looked at her mother.

'Leave it.' Miranda switched on the ansaphone. The machine clicked and Gordon's disembodied voice spilt thinly from the small speaker. Miranda had lost the booklet with the seven-step procedure required to change the message. At the beginning she had enjoyed the irony of it. Having Gordon still answer the phone was one of the few signals she could send to the world of her resilience. She almost hoped that Gordon would call and have to talk to his other self.

'. . . so if you'd like to leave a message, then please do it, do so, after the tone. If not then . . . then please feel free, ah, not to. Either way, thanks for –' At this point the tone cut in, and an unfamiliar voice took his place.

'Miranda. Stephen Graham speaking. Calling to see how you are. That's all. I didn't quite get the gist last night. Piran hadn't told me. I wish he had but there you are. There's no need to call back. Unless you want to. In which case I'm at the shop.' He left a number and signed off.

'I met him,' Miranda said, guilty for no good reason she could think of, 'last night, he was at the party.' No good reason except for the fact that he was a man. Not a man who mattered. But if Gordon didn't come back then there could easily be calls from men who mattered. So the guilt was perhaps foreshadowing what she would feel.

'He sounded nice,' Pen said, trying out the notion of stepfatherdom for herself. It left her cold.

'Yes. He rides a bicycle.' Miranda automatically reached for something she knew would endear him to Pen. She had picked up his cycle clips with the intention of returning them to him and apologising. It wasn't his fault Gordon had left. Neither was it Anne's, who had now rung and was apologising tearfully into the ansaphone.

'. . . know how you feel, I mean, can't imagine. But one assumes because you've always seemed so . . . well–adjusted that you didn't need us. I should have been a better friend. I'm sorry. I can't imagine how I would feel if it happened to me . . .'

Ben walked into the kitchen in his pyjamas.

'I need a wee wee.' He was carrying a red beaker. It was upside down. 'The water fallded out,' he said, looking into the empty cup. Miranda shooed him from the room and up the stairs. He mounted the lavatory with gusto via a plastic step and sat on the seat, slumped slightly forwards, his hands in his lap. He was capable of using the lavatory on his own but preferred an audience. 'I can do this,' he said, pushing his penis into the gap between the seat and the rim of the bowl with his finger.

'That's good, darling,' Miranda patronised fondly. 'Have you finished?'

'No. I need a pooh I do.' As Ben strained joyously Miranda decided to do something with her day. When she'd dropped the children off she'd go and buy a book from Stephen.

THREE

GORDON WAS SITTING in a small wooden hut overlooking a lake. He was thinking, as he often did, of home. On the night he had left Gordon had tried sleeping out in the park round the corner from the house, but it was too cold. He'd always imagined there to be a certain nobility in life on the road. He had soon realised there was none. Everything he had taken for granted suddenly needed serious consideration. Even going to the lavatory had to be plotted an hour or so in advance. Civilisation, he now knew, was not central heating, a weekly trip to Asda, and a couple of weeks abroad in the summer. It was unrestricted access to running hot and cold water, toilet paper and an unblocked toilet with a seat.

He had left the bench at three a.m. and gone in search of warmth. He had found it, briefly, on Victoria station, but was soon moved on. He'd then walked down to the Embankment. Each shop door with sufficient legroom was filled by the cardboard-layered bedding of street dwellers. Every promised area of warmth had been locked tight, every bright arcade barred by adolescent uniformed security guards. When the sun came up he had slept on a bench by Westminster Bridge. He was woken shortly afterwards by a clutch of grinning Japanese tourists thrusting a camera towards him and gesticulating that he take their picture against the backdrop of Big Ben. Gordon had caught the Underground home, let himself in, showered, changed and slept for an hour in front of the television. Miranda was out. The children were at school.

Gordon had then left home for a second time. This time he was more prepared. He had rummaged through the loft until he found an old sleeping bag and rucksack which he filled with blankets, clean clothes, thick socks and tinned tuna. He had picked up a waterproof coat, packed his old walking boots, and set off for the motorway. He'd stopped on the way to ring Clive from a public pay-phone.

'Clive. Gordon.'

'Oh, hello . . .'

'Don't talk. Just listen. My money's running out. Right? Now, I'm on my way north. I've left Miranda.'

Clive had tried to interject, but Gordon cut him off.

'When I get where I'm going, I'm going to call you. And you're going to send me some money. I know you can afford it. You're going to send me enough to survive. No more. Right? And then I won't bother troubling either Piran or Anne with the truth about Sandy and you. That's it. I'm not pissed off with you, not as pissed off as I should be actually, considering we were supposed to be friends. But I reckon you owe me. That's it. I'll let you know where you can contact me.'

And when Gordon had got where he was going he had contacted Clive, and Clive had dutifully paid for Gordon's bed and breakfast life as, over the first month, he had moved through the Midlands, up to the North-east, crossed over to Liverpool, then completed the triangle and settled in comfortable digs just north of Derby. The city had a library and nobody knew him. And there Gordon stayed. He had supposed for a while that he was having a breakdown, but he wasn't. He was having a holiday from his responsibilities and the only contacts he made with the world were his occasional letters to Pen and a carefully written note to Chunder in which he asked for his job to be kept open. Miraculously, Chunder had agreed. He had given him six months. A sort of semi maternity leave. That's how Gordon rationalised it as he settled into his new life.

The guilt was manageable. It worsened each evening when he imagined Pen and Ben being put to bed. It lessened for a while after each letter. He was never entirely happy with the letters. He had begun by sending Pen a series of ridiculous vignettes of life on the road with Professor Bunyan. But these, he realised, were solely for his own entertainment. He had also tried to write to Miranda, but these letters never made it past the statutory cooling-off period between finishing and sending them. He was sorry. She knew that. He was a coward for running. She didn't need to be told that. He had no money to send her. That was self-evident. And he still loved her. That she would never believe. So he didn't write and, instead, decided to phone. He gave this up after the first visit to the phone box. The same arguments held. The important thing was for him to be in contact with his old life and the financial connection with Clive was sufficient for that. Clive, after the first few weeks, had taken to dropping a few lines to let him know how things were. So he was in touch, in a way; at least as in touch as he wanted to be.

After two months he had found himself the part-time job in a park. The park, which was close to his digs, had a large boating lake with two small, lightly treed islands in it. Rowing boats were hired out on an hourly basis and Gordon got the job of letting them out. He earned two pounds a session. He had a small green wooden hut to shelter in.

Inside was a small oil-fired stove, a bench and a blackboard onto which he could chalk the time each boat had been taken. When it rained, Gordon would close up the hut, and through a small window watch the rain driving into the lake. Gordon found that he looked forward to the rainy days more than the sunny ones because he soon came to realise that he didn't actually need human contact at all. The cursory conversations with Mrs Hill, his landlady, Mrs Hill the elder, her mother, and Mr Blake, the care-in-the-community man, who was the only other lodger, were all he required.

It was raining today. Gordon had the glazed window shut and was watching the lake. The lake had become choked with weeds and the rowers often complained that much of it was impossible to row on. Gordon was working out how he could put forward a strong enough case to have the lake dredged. He was even prepared to do it himself if the council allowed it. After weeks without his usual concerns, he found his mind had a habit of seizing on schemes which would be of benefit to the wider community. Gordon was also composing his latest letter to Pen. He always wrote with the stub of a pencil he had brought with him from home. An HB pencil. The letter was on the bench beneath the blackboard among a scattering of old boat-hire tickets. The paper was dry and crisp because Gordon had lit the stove. He lit the stove at every opportunity because it made the hut more cosy. The warmer the hut became, the happier Gordon was. A couple walking arm-in-arm, oblivious to the rain, watched him from the edge of the lake. They saw an unshaven man with a strange light playing behind his eyes. But there was something unsettling about him. He was at rest but not at peace.

Mrs Hill kept cats and budgerigars. She seemed to enjoy the tension that existed between them. The cats waited beneath the cages. The budgerigars twittered and chattered insanely into their bells and mirrors. Mr Blake, the care-in-the-community man, called the birds his trapped blue angels and was forever opening the cages. He stamped on the cats with his size thirteen shoes whenever they came close. Mrs Hill seemed to have no existence outside the house. Gordon never saw her leave or return from anywhere and yet she always claimed to have had 'adventures' when they talked each evening over tea, which was always taken on trays in the front lounge at 4.30. There was no 'back' lounge. Mrs Hill's philosophy on food was that the quantities should diminish throughout the day. She did not, however, provide a cooked breakfast, and lunch was to be taken out. 'Tea' was wafer-thin white bread, a saucer of ham between them and a large brown pot of tea. Mr Blake took his lunch in the nearby precinct. He left the house at ten thirty each day. He then sat in the library until 12.15 at which time he would buy a meat pie which he would eat standing up by the charity shop, then return to the house at 3.15. His routine was unvarying except for the periods in which he forgot to take his medication when he would be found preaching loudly about the perils of protein in the town centre.

Gordon was more than happy with the set-up. It appealed to his sense of the absurd. Mrs Hill's tidy pebble-dashed semi and her routines reminded him of childhood Sundays at his grandmother's house. By rights those Sundays he spent with his grandmother should have been torture to a small boy. She had no games or properly functioning television. Her record player was broken and her house was cold and dark. But Gordon filled the gaps with his imagination. The cellar was always full of apples piled against the wall and smelt like summer all through the winter. In another corner was a pile of potatoes on sacking. Paint was stacked on the shelves, the whitewashed walls were coated in coal dust. The brick floor was gritty with bits of cold coal. Through the grating at the front he could see up women's dresses as they walked by, a persistent urge provoking a nagging thrill he only later understood. The steps to the kitchen were steep and treacherous and lit by a naked swinging bulb which he always thought of when he watched the opening credits to *Callan*. Gordon spent half the day in the cellar and the other half in the upstairs part of the house, which his grandmother never used on account of her rheumatism. In the back bedroom, more cobwebby and interesting each time he went, was the thick family Bible in a wardrobe. In the front small room was a dusty single bed and a Noddy lampshade which his grandfather had put up for him when he first spent the night there.

Gordon was happy at his grandmother's house and he began to wonder whether it was because he had been happy there that he stayed with Mrs Hill.

Mrs Hill the elder's dignity was often preserved only by the intercessions of her daughter, but it didn't matter, she was a benign presence.

'Will you be eating th'ham, Mr Meadows?' Mrs Hill's language was subject to random conflations, her peculiar turns of phrase the result of a Catholic taste in TV soaps.

'No, please, you have it.' Gordon had lost his appetite almost entirely. Even one slice of transparent meat had become too much. He pushed the saucer across the table. Mr Blake eyed him warily, afraid the extra slice would end up on his plate. Blake was a large, powerful man, with voluminous eyebrows that hung like moss over his unwelcoming eyes. He carried himself as if he was afraid of his strength. Gordon felt as though there were two people in Blake's body, a giant and a small child who chaperoned him. When his expression did change, it reconfigured into something childlike; his curiosities were fleeting but often filled with wonder.

Blake's meals were ritualised to the extent that anything beyond what he expected threw out his routine for days. His equilibrium was perilously balanced. Christmas lunch, which was the one mid-day meal taken at the house, was planned well in advance in his spotless bedroom. Gordon had once, out of pure nosiness, looked into Mr Blake's room when he'd gone to the precinct. The bed was immaculately made. There was a child's school desk, a blue exercise book, a Bible and a fountain pen. The wardrobe held three white shirts, one spare pair of blue trousers, one spare cardigan and Mr Blake's mac.

'You'll have it, Mother,' Mrs Hill insisted, folding Gordon's unwanted slice of ham and pushing it between the old woman's teeth. Mrs Hill the elder chewed glumly and silently. She rarely spoke except when there was rugby on the television at which she chanted rhythmically and often urinated with excitement onto the armchair. Mrs Hill had now taken to covering her chair with a groundsheet.

'Any adventures today, Mrs Hill?' Gordon prompted.

'Adventures you wouldn't believe, Mr Meadows.' She gave her stock response.

'Marvellous. Isn't it, Mr Blake?'

'M . . . marvellous,' Blake muttered.

'I hope I'm that active when I ah . . .' Gordon backed off. Mrs Hill was of indeterminate age. She could have been anything from fifty to sixty-five. But she prided herself on her corseted, handsome appearance. Her hair received the majority of her attention. The style would have been called a bee-hive thirty years before.

'And how was the hut today?' Mrs Hill said.

'Quiet. Very quiet. I had a courting couple . . .'

'In the rain!'

'They didn't seem to notice it. They took a boat out for an hour.'

'Not on to the island!'

'On to the island.'

Mrs Hill the elder broke wind.

'Do you want the toilet, Mother?'

'Too late. You're too late,' the old woman announced with glee.

'Fetch me the pot, Mr Meadows.' Gordon fetched the pot from its hook in the kitchen. It was still raining. The night was coming, he needed to finish the letter to Pen and get it off before the morning. He had wanted to write about Mrs Hill and Mr Blake but he knew she'd never believe him.

In the evening, Gordon took a break from his habit of reading in his room, and walked into town. He rarely spent Clive's allowance on leisure activities but he realised as he had dated Pen's sixth letter that he had been away three months to the day and felt the occasion deserved marking in some way. He had never been bored in this time, just empty and cold. And he had not touched alcohol since the night he left. He would have a bottle of Bass.

At a little after midnight he woke on a bench in the market place. He was depressed and tearful and whatever dam had been keeping his feelings for home at bay had burst. He phoned home but slammed the phone down in shock when he heard his own voice asking him to leave a message. He could remember only one other number. He dialled it and Anne answered. Her voice was drowned momentarily by the sound of a police car chasing up the street towards the cathedral. He tried to say what he wanted to say but realised he had no idea of what it was he had called for. So he apologised to Miranda and rang off.

When he got back to Mrs Hill's she had bolted the door, so he went to his hut, lit the stove and slept soundly by the silent lake.

FOUR

STEPHEN'S BOOKSHOP WAS disappointingly modern. Miranda had imagined him to own a tall and narrow Dickensian establishment with bottle-bottomed windows, thousands of calf-backed volumes and a set of steps with casters that he would punt round the shelves looking for obscure volumes. Instead she found him to be the deputy manager of one of the branches of a nationwide chain. The shop was hushed and had wide tables supporting neat piles of high-gloss hardbacks. Mozart was piped almost inaudibly from the hidden speakers. The lighting was diffused and bathed the honey-coloured wood shelves with ersatz daylight. Books were offered with apologies for the price; the assistants it seemed would give them away if they could. Literature may have been the currency but civilisation was the commodity that was being traded.

Stephen was at a high-tech till island in the centre of the shop. He had his head bowed into a book. Miranda approached him across the abundant carpet and he looked up only as she got to the desk.

'Oh,' he said, and blushed as he carefully closed a thin paperback.

'Yes, I've brought your . . .' Miranda was equally fazed.

She delved into her handbag for the cycle clips and as she pulled them out found one had clamped her packet of tampons in its measly jaws. '. . . cycle clips.' She shook the clip from the packet and slipped it back into her handbag.

'Thank you. Yes. Thank you so much.' Stephen's blush faded into a pasty white as he pushed the clips into the torn pocket of his tweed jacket. He was better-looking than Miranda remembered; she realised she had barely given him a second glance the night before, her attention had been centred on another part of the room. She was surprised to find herself now quite attracted to him.

Stephen was, as she remembered, lean, but his narrow face was guileless. He reminded her of the figures she had seen in a photograph of a group of young men on a farm cart who were setting off to join up in 1914. None of the nine men in the photograph had come home and there was something in their expression that suggested to Miranda that they seemed to have an idea of what their fates might be.

'I suppose I came to apologise,' Miranda said, knowing full well that she hadn't.

'Absolutely no need. Please.'

'Well, thank you anyway . . .' She wanted to stay and sensed that Stephen wanted her to stay but she could think of no reason to.

'Wretched situation,' Stephen said.

'Is it?'

'Yours, I mean. The, ah, your, ah, husband shooting off like that.'

'We manage. No sympathy required,' she said firmly.

'Fine. Understood.'

'What are you reading?'

Stephen pulled out the book from a shelf below the counter and handed it to her. 'Guy de Maupassant.'

'He died of syphilis. Didn't he?' It was the first fact that sprang to her mind about him. Miranda had a card index of such facts in her head and only by expressing the headline could she then access the rest of the information she carried. It was an unconventional system but it had earned her a decent degree.

'I suppose he did.' Stephen took the book back and laid it face down on the counter. She had disappointed him – or he had become disappointed with the book, Miranda couldn't tell.

'I remember . . . the sailboat. The family. Two brothers . . .'

'That's right,' Stephen prompted.

'And something about the boat going through the water like a plough through a field. I think I'll always remember that.'

'Yes. Of course.' Stephen picked up the book again, his belief in it – or her – restored.

'I suppose you don't fancy lunch, do you?'

'Well . . .' Stephen looked at his watch.

'Oh, it doesn't matter. I suppose you're busy at such short notice.'

'No. It's not that, it's just . . .'

'Really. Please. It doesn't matter. Another time.'

'No. It's just. I have to, ah, fetch my laundry. That's all. It won't take a minute.'

'Oh. Fine. Well. Where shall we meet?'

Stephen gave the matter some consideration. He seemed to imagine that in doing so Miranda would consider him spoilt for choice: as if he lunched somewhere different each day. The truth, as she immediately realised, was that he never went out and took his sandwiches in the windowless stock room in the basement of the store.

They decided, as Stephen's break was only ten minutes away, that Miranda would wait. While she waited, she browsed, aware that Stephen was watching her. Despite the fact that he was a rather peculiar specimen, Miranda enjoyed the attention.

At twelve-thirty they walked round the corner to the launderette. The establishment, littered with odd socks and soap powder packets, was anomalous in the crowded narrow street of otherwise sleek, smoke-glassed advertising agencies, Vietnamese restaurants and minimalist art galleries. Expensive cars were double-parked blinking their hazard lights; motor-bike messengers hurried packages into air-conditioned interiors after shouting into corroded entryphones. It was a street that knew where it was going. Stephen pointed to the second-floor window of his flat; it was above an architect's office. A display of blood-red geraniums showed from a terracotta trough perched with no visible sign of attachment on a window ledge.

Miranda waited outside the launderette but couldn't resist watching as Stephen fumbled the saturated grey octopus of his clothes into the belly of the dryer. He fumbled for his change, looked at his watch, slotted in a series of fifty pence coins and turned a gnarled silver knob. The machine rotated and pitched the heavy sodden mass from top to bottom once, twice, then picked up speed and the clothes were free to gambol in the darkness.

'There. Ah.' On coming out, Stephen offered his arm in a quaint but unconscious gesture of gallantry and Miranda took it in the same spirit.

'How long do you have?'

'Oh. Ages.' He looked at his watch. 'I asked the woman to bag the clothes for me. It's a service they provide for thirty-five pence. You can have a full service wash for a pound, but I prefer to measure the powder in myself. That way . . .'

'Ssh,' Miranda tugged his arm closer. 'It's alright not to

talk, you know. We're not, I mean, it's not as though we're out on a date or anything.'

'Of course not.'

They had sandwiches in the Lamb and Flag. Miranda drank gin and Stephen ordered a pint of Guinness. There was no discomfort between them except for the moment when she mentioned Gordon's letters and he attempted a reading of his motives for using hieroglyphics. Miranda snapped a short retort and they fell silent until her regret prompted a conciliatory: 'I like the street. It's rather bohemian, isn't it?' It wasn't an observation she would normally have been comfortable in making, but Stephen's odd, slightly strangulated poshness seemed to call out for such statements.

'Yes. I can't say I'm in favour of the changes, but I suppose one should be glad to have tenants who pay promptly.'

'Tenants?'

'Yes.'

'So you own . . . I mean, you let out rooms in your flat, do you?'

'No. I mean the restaurant over there, the architects, that ironmongers, the launderette and a couple of others, oh . . .' He waved towards the end of the street. 'That way.'

'I see,' Miranda said, tugging Stephen's arm a little closer.

FIVE

ANNE AND CLIVE lived in a cul-de-sac of imposing but stark detached houses which had been built during the 1930s. Miranda called round there on the way home. The road was unadopted which meant that it was pot-holed, tar-patched and stone-chipped. The chippings had been scattered across the narrow grassed verges which vaguely and politely defined the front boundaries of each property. Beyond these were the more serious emblems of ownership: a variety of fences, then the lawns, then the tall cliff-like façades of the houses, supporting sharply pitched lichen-chalked roofs. Despite these natural and man-made obstacles to entry, each house also had a collection of strategically placed movement-sensing spotlights and bright coloured alarm boxes. Anne and Clive lived at the furthest and darkest end of the road, the trees increasing in density the further along you went. Miranda buzzed the entryphone on the post of the five-bar gate. From the metal box, Anne issued the instruction for her to come in. Something clicked and triggered the gate to swing inwards.

They sat on white metal garden furniture beside the covered swimming pool. The back garden was extensive, laid to lawn and dotted with bright new stone statues and statuettes, pillars and half pillars that Clive had recently bought from the local garden centre. Where the lawn-mower's blades had failed to reach, each plinth had a tiny vertical fringe of grass. Clive had also wired the garden with coloured lanterns which were currently switched on. This had the effect of making Miranda feel as though she was hallucinating, as the heart of each tree glowed orange, red or green.

'Ghastly, isn't it?' Anne said as if she was seeing the garden for the first time.

'Garish; I suppose that's the word. Not as bad as you think. Really, it's not,' Miranda offered tactfully.

'Once Clive has an idea in his tiny little mind it's pointless arguing with him. I mean, I used to go with him on his spending sprees. At least then I could moderate his wilder excesses of kitsch. I don't bother any more. I suppose I'm working on the principle that if I don't rise to the bait then he'll stop doing it. It wouldn't be so bad if he was doing it with a sense of humour.' Anne was in a reflective mood; the tone of her words was uncharacteristically gentle. If she hadn't been bad-mouthing Clive, Miranda could almost have believed that they were talking about love.

'Look, I'm sorry about this morning . . .'

Anne held up her hand. 'No. You were perfectly within your rights.'

'Even so.'

'I think we've known each other long enough for us to let moments like that pass.' Anne stood up and put her empty glass on the table. 'Walk with me.' She held out her arm. 'Round the estate,' she added as if she couldn't quite let the intimacy of the gesture go without some mockery.

Miranda checked her watch. She still had an hour before she had to get back to pick Ben up so she took Anne's ample, pitted arm and let herself be led on a slow meandering walk that took in each of Clive's statues. The detail on them was exemplary. Some Anne had christened with names of people that she knew: Piran and Sandy were a Mary and Joseph grouping cradling a mewling Jesus. Others were characters she'd invented on her long afternoons alone. Despite trying hard to stop herself, Miranda was fast re-appraising indiscreet, capable Anne. She now saw a rather directionless, almost self-pitying figure, wandering like a nun round a graveyard.

They stopped beside a small murky fishpond. Flashes of carrot gold tousled the dense brown weeds; a fountain trickled a puny thread of water into a stone birdbath. On the far side of the pond there were two more stone figures, green with age: a small boy kneeling beside the pond, a small girl standing self-consciously beside a stone dog. Behind them the garden melted into an impenetrable and threatening darkness, towered over by a selection of mature trees.

'They were there when we came,' Anne said, looking pointedly at the statues as if she were searching for signs of life. 'I like them being there. I need your advice.' She strung the thoughts together so that it was a second before Miranda realised she'd been called upon to respond.

'Yes. Of course. What is it?' She had hoped that Anne would lead them back to the house. This shaded, damp corner of the garden had rather unsettling overtones.

'I think Clive's having an affair.'

'Oh.' Miranda couldn't help it, she'd never be able to make the necessary response to that word again.

'I suppose it's unfair of me to burden you with this.' Anne waited, but Miranda didn't disagree. 'However. However, I need a . . . just another view on it really. It could be complete paranoia, but then . . .'

'But then look what happened to me,' Miranda said quickly.

'No. That's not what I was going to say.'

'I'm sorry.'

'I was going to say that it wouldn't have been the first time.'

'Ah.'

'Except this time I think it's a little more serious.'

'Yes?' Miranda had been gloom-free since lunch, something she realised only as the darkness descended on her once more.

'He's sending her money. About two hundred a month. I picked it up on the statements: he never puts the payee on the cheque stubs.'

'That's rather careless, isn't it? Leaving the statements around, I mean.'

'Not at all. He has a quaint view of our financial affairs. He somehow believes that because he's the one with the penis, he's the only one who can balance the books. It's all in his drawer marked "accounts". His father was the organised one in his family. Clive and he are both able to compartmentalise their lives – which I imagine must be necessary if one is having an affair. That's not to say I don't like his father because I do.'

'Well, what will you do?'

'I don't know. Really I don't know. I wouldn't want to lose him.' Anne reached out and touched Miranda's arm in a sudden gesture of apology. You had to be so careful nowadays.

'Then have it out with him. You can't just ignore it.'

'Do you know something?'

'What?' Miranda turned to see Anne blushing.

'I sometimes imagine him with somebody else. You know . . .'

'Screwing them, you mean.'

'Yes.'

'And?'

'I despise him for it. I despise him for the humiliation. But it ... it excites me. I don't know whether it is the humiliation or ... I don't know, it's something about power, isn't it. With him it has always been about power. I can't bear him near me. But at the same time ...'

There was a call from the house. Clive briefly appeared on the patio in his immaculate, themed leisurewear. Seeing Miranda was there, he waved the empty wine bottle in the air, mimed that he was going to fetch another, then disappeared back into the house.

'Ask him,' Miranda said.

'Should I?'

'Yes. Ask him now. While I'm here.'

'You hard-faced bitch.'

'You must be prepared to take pleasure where you can find it.'

'That sounds like good advice.'

'Yes. It was.' Miranda had been caught off guard.

'From somebody I know?'

'Yes.'

'Do you ever fantasise?' Anne said, kneeling at the pond's edge and tugging at the dense weeds. She laid each handful down in a neat pile.

'I used to.'

'But not now?'

'Fantasy is an escape from mundane reality, isn't it? Whatever my life is now, it is no longer mundane.'

But Miranda had already found herself fantasising about Stephen and she continued to do so as they waited in silence for Clive. Soon he was zigzagging across the lawn towards them, clowning with his tray of wine and glasses as though he were a waiter on the deck of a pitching ship. The women waited for him to reach them beside the fish pond, each

hoping to gain something for themselves in Clive's humiliation.

SIX

WHEN GORDON TURNED up Mrs Hill's short steep drive, the first thing he saw was Mr Blake standing at the living-room window. His image was fragmented by the diamond-leaded panes which made him look like a museum exhibit in a display case. Gordon waved. He had slept soundly in the hut by the lake and he knew that a night away from Mrs Hill's had done him good. Mr Blake looked back inscrutably. Seeing Gordon had arrived home safely, he went to fetch his coat. His routine had settled back to normal. Gordon let himself in round the back. Mrs Hill was beside the breakfast table wiping her mother's face with a green flannel. Mrs Hill the elder was complaining loudly at the lack of tenderness her daughter was showing but, even so, her face remained coated with dried porridge.

'Morning,' Gordon said brightly, closing the door behind him.

'Where've you been?' Mrs Hill the elder started and stared at him glassily.

'Come in, Mr Meadows. Ignore Mother, she hasn't had her tablets. Sit yourself down. I'll fetch your toast.'

'Thanks.' Gordon was glad to be back within range of Mrs Hill's capable compass but, having left it for a while, already knew that it was time to leave for good. He sat down opposite the dishevelled figure of his landlady's mother. Her bitter eyes, not comprehending her loss of dignity, were sunken. Her ageing head always seemed browner and more shrivelled in the morning. She had a flame-red dressing gown on and the ensemble put Gordon in mind of a potato being baked on a bonfire.

'Been tomcatting have you?' Mrs Hill the elder leered. She clenched her fist and approximated a feeble, half-remembered obscene gesture.

'Yes, Mrs Hill, I've been taking my pleasure with the landlady's daughter.' Gordon retrieved the marmaladed copy of the *Daily Mail* from beneath the tea pot. 'Dipping my wick.'

'Dirty bugger.'

'Ignore him, Mother. Mr Meadows is teasing you. Aren't you, Mr Meadows?'

'Ah . . . yes. Yes, I suppose I am.'

'I won't apologise for locking the door last night, Mr Meadows. I'm sure you'll appreciate the necessity to abide by the house rules.'

'Yes. Of course.'

'Otherwise Mr Blake might start getting ideas and before you know it, he'll be back inside the hospital. The mentally ill need to keep regular hours as I'm sure you appreciate.'

'Dirty Pole!' Mrs Hill the elder shouted and, in her excitement, broke wind.

'No, that was the man before Mr Meadows, Mother. We had a Pole in before you, Mr Meadows. I'm afraid I had to let him leave on account of certain breaches of my hygiene regulations. There you are.' Mrs Hill put a saucer of thin toast on the table. One corner was glossed with melted margarine, it was otherwise bone-dry. Gordon looked round for the marmalade jar but it had been put away. He prised a small but stubborn lump of orange peel from the sports page of the *Mail* and wiped it onto his toast. The bitterness was welcome against the charcoal taste of the burnt bread.

'Is it alright for you, then?' Mrs Hill hovered like a maître d' at a banquet.

'A feast, Mrs Hill.' Gordon knew he should never had spent the night away. He felt as though he had woken after a long and deep sleep. For the first time since leaving, he had dreamt of home.

'Could I trouble you for your crockery?' Mrs Hill said and Gordon handed over his saucer. The toast had been on it for less than a minute.

'I think I'm going to have to leave you, Mrs Hill.'

'For the lake?'

'No. For pastures new, I'm afraid.' Another spur to moving on was that Gordon had become aware of a slow transmutation taking place. One of the first books he read after leaving home was *The History of Mr Polly*. Having temporarily misplaced a number of his most familiar character traits – self-deprecating humour, cynicism, world-weariness, mild alcoholism – he was aware of having commandeered some of those that Wells had ascribed to his chipper creation.

'Heavens.' Mrs Hill stood rigid at the sink.

'Good riddance to you,' her mother sniped.

'I'll give you a week's notice. I think that's the house rule, isn't it?'

'Mother shall be sorry to see you go.' Mrs Hill continued to scour the pots. 'She would have liked you. When she was herself.'

'I'm sorry. I mean, not sorry, I mean, it's unfortunate that you have to spend so much of your time looking after her.'

'It's a burden I gladly bear, Mr Meadows. The folks who

cast off their burdens are the ones who let themselves get carried away.'

'Yes. Of course.' Gordon made a mental note. He had a small notebook of Mrs Hill's homilies in his room.

'Perhaps, if you could spare the time, you would join me for a sweet sherry when Mother has gone down. Say tomorrow, about nine-thirty. After the weather?'

'I'd like that.'

Gordon walked back to the park. Mrs Hill's mood had altered dramatically after he'd given his notice; she'd even slapped her mother's arm when she tipped her tea on to the floor. The older woman looked at the angry mark first with surprise, then with shock. Like a child, she licked her thumb and tried to wipe it away. Mrs Hill watched her sadly; it was rare for her to allow her mother's antics to go as far as to induce pathos.

Gordon sat outside the hut by the boating lake and rolled a cigarette; handrolling tobacco was a re-discovered pleasure. He rationed himself to three slim roll-ups a day and savoured each inhalation. The smoke pitched him back in time to the university, to the perpetual, endless afternoons when he and Sandy would study together. Or at least that was always the intention. The reality was that they'd talk, and smoke Old Holborn, and listen to Jefferson Airplane. Somehow he'd lost himself there; a part of him had become detached and been shunted off into a siding. He wondered if it wasn't something to do with Sandy. Perhaps she held the missing part of him, or perhaps she was just a witness to a time when, however major his responsibilities seemed, they were never greater than completing an essay or turning up on time to a lecture.

The corollary of growing up, having children and paying the mortgage seemed to be a loss of any possibility of doing anything solely for his own pleasure. But now, of course, he'd gone too far and he was in his own eyes, a rather pathetic specimen: a middle-aged man, who'd run away from home and was sitting by a wide and beautiful lake, smoking the cigarettes he'd smoked as a teenager and dreaming of a life he now considered to be the model of perfection. But it wasn't perfect. Despite having met Sandy, he had been alone for much of the time, and utterly miserable. So how far back did he have to go to find what he was looking for? Perhaps to the child he'd re-incarnated in his grandmother's house. That child was alone, but also happy – certainly content. Before that there was just a real child like Ben, who never questioned happiness, he simply took it. In trying to be honest with himself, Gordon recognised that he resented Ben. He was uncomfortable with his unconscious displays of emotion. He felt more affinity with Pen; with pensive, solitary Pen: a child he'd created in his own image – somehow; unintentionally. Perhaps the route to what he was looking for lay with his children.

Gordon looked across the lake; the island was mirrored in the still water. The unveiled sky seemed vaster than the one back home. He knew that nature held some kind of message for him; each time he stood in awe of it he was aware of the implicit symbolism: something that was written into the slowness of the currents, in the height and angles of the hills. Marvelling at the beauty of it all just got in the way of real understanding. Perhaps one day he'd see it.

Something caught Gordon's attention on the far bank. It was a figure in a gabardine mac standing stone-still and staring at him through a pair of binoculars. Gordon waved when he recognised the figure as Mr Blake. Mr Blake did not wave back but, having been spotted, let his binoculars drop heavily to his chest and set off for the precinct. He was simply checking that Gordon was still there, but his routine was already in tatters.

SEVEN

Miranda called Stephen the following day. She had intended to thank him for lunch but knew this was just a pretext for speaking to him again. When he offered she readily accepted his invitation to meet again in the Lamb and Flag. It was Stephen's half day and, after lunch, they walked arm-in-arm round the corner to his flat. After a brief preamble they were in his bed. It wasn't sex, not in the fullest sense because Miranda had her period, but it was as close to it as they could manage. Stephen had a surprisingly good body. He 'worked out' three times a week, and it showed in the firm corrugations of his abdominal muscles which Miranda reached for as she cupped and nuzzled him beneath the duvet. As she did so, he was reaching down to massage her shoulders. He began by taking her naked neck like a strangler; his thumbs to her throat, his fingers yoking her shoulders. Then he kneaded her tenseness, picking up the rhythm from her bobbing head. The bed was an inferno and when they had finished Miranda threw off the sheets and knelt at the foot of it. Stephen lay unselfconsciously naked, his legs a little splayed, and Miranda tried to read the expression on his face. It was more than contentment. It was almost smugness.

'You have wonderful legs,' Miranda said, leaning towards him and fondling his thighs.

'Thank you,' Stephen said.

Miranda climbed up his body and straddled him. She took his hands and placed them on her breasts. 'I thought this was revenge . . .'

'Yes?'

'And then I undressed you and it wasn't.' Feeling his hands on her she felt a sharp desire that connected the circuit from her ears to her breasts to her womb to the small of her back. 'I needed this. I needed to be needed.'

'I do need you.'

'I didn't . . . I mean, Christ we've only known each other for two days; why do I feel able to talk to you like this?'

'It happens.'

'I didn't think I was capable of feeling like this. With Gor . . . Before, it was, sex, I mean, it was a chore. Something to be got out of the way. I never really wanted it. No, this is too . . . I just want to say that what I feel now I didn't think I was capable of feeling.' But she had felt it. Or, at least she had been given a clue to it one lunchtime in a hotel with a man who, declaring himself to be a Catholic, kissed her and wouldn't stop. Even when she told him to. She had never regretted not going upstairs with him. She would never have been able to face him again. Even now when she saw him it was awkward. How the quiet woman put up with him she would never know.

But thoughts of the quiet man didn't belong here, in this new, narrow dimension she had found with Stephen, and she wanted to enjoy it while she could. Miranda's relationships had, until Gordon, always resolved like the horror film dénouements in which the spiked walls close in, threatening to crush the victim. Of course the victim always escapes at the final moment, as did she. With Stephen she felt it would be different.

After the previous day's revelation about his wealth, further reappraisals had become necessary when Miranda saw Stephen's flat. The flat was two storeys high, but someone with a keen eye on the centre-spread of an architectural journal had removed the intervening floor and created a cathedral-like space of bare brick and metal, spiral stairs and balconied bedrooms. The kitchen, which Stephen was inordinately proud of, seemed to have been modelled on an operating theatre. Miranda trailed her hands across the pristine stainless-steel surfaces, marvelling at the lack of dust and clutter. How much of Stephen had gone into the design of the flat was hard to tell. He was habitually evasive: whether it was in response to her questions about his background, the identity of the two intertwined naked women photographed in black and white and framed above his bed, or the bizarre contradiction of his wealth and his job in the bookshop, Stephen always seemed to manage to turn the question back on her.

'Tell me about your family,' she tried again as they lay on his bed.

'Oh, I don't know,' Stephen sighed, 'My mother and father are dead. I have a sister with a brood – somewhere.'

'Somewhere?'

'Australia when last I heard. They were going out to farm – or something. My father farmed. Some of the time, anyway.'

'And you inherited all this, the property, I mean, did you?'

'No. I was lucky. I bought and sold at the right time. My father advised me. I suppose you could consider that to be an inheritance . . . Can I get you anything?'

'No. Nothing. Just stay where you are and don't move an inch.'

'Do we finish now? I mean, is this all?' Stephen said.

'What do you mean?'

'I'm not quite sure where I stand.'

'Oh, I see. You mean you think I'm just here for the sex or something, do you?'

'I don't think I said that, did I?' Stephen sat up, forcing Miranda to move her head from the pillow of his breast-bone.

'Do you want us to finish?' Miranda's first thought had been of Pen; following that, just how long Gordon had been gone. Then she realised how little she had done for herself in the past three months, or, perhaps, even longer. Yes. Definitely longer.

'No.'

'Then, no. Not by any means,' she said, slightly puzzled that she had to explain it to him. After all, what did he think she was telling him after they had made love?

'Good.'

'You're not attached, are you? I never thought to ask.'

'Do you think you'd be here if I was?'

'I don't know.' Miranda looked at the photograph on the wall. Any man who would display his conquests so proudly would be capable of anything; except, perhaps, honesty. 'They're very beautiful, your women.'

'Yes. They are.'

Miranda felt an irritating surge of jealousy. 'Do they have names?'

'Yes. The taller woman is called Beatrice. The other is called Mary. Do you see any family resemblance?'

Miranda switched her attention quickly back to Stephen. 'With Beatrice, perhaps.'

'Yes. She had quite perfect features, didn't she?'

'You broke up?'

'In a manner of speaking. She was my mother.'

Pen arrived home from school and let herself into the house. Although she didn't mind returning to an empty home she never relaxed until she'd looked into all of the rooms to make sure there was nobody there. If she didn't go upstairs immediately, her fears of what might be lying in wait on the first floor escalated so quickly that she then had to wait for her mother to arrive home before she even allowed herself to go to the toilet. She'd picked up her father's latest letter from the mat and she tore it open as she sat down on her bed. A small blue ticket dropped out of the envelope. A moment later she was in tears. She balled the letter and threw it at the map of Egypt on the wall. Then she went over and tore the map down. Gordon had reached Cairo but he was travelling on. This wasn't the arrangement. He was supposed to be coming straight home; they'd agreed.

The hot, self-pitying tears that burnt down Pen's face were accompanied by an ache in her chest. She was hurt and humiliated. She had not cried since the night her father left, she had lost her trust in him and, for a while, her entire faith in humanity. For a second she found herself thinking of Connie Monnery; she now knew something of what she felt. You had to be strong to exist solely on your faith in yourself. Pen didn't yet feel old enough for that.

Her eye was caught by the blue ticket on the floor. It had the name of a city council on it, a crest, the name of a park and a time: 3.20. It was almost as if her father was calling for her to come to him. There was only one option open to her now. She packed a small bag, changed into her black jeans and warm jumper, emptied the brown envelope in the desk drawer of money and, following in her father's footsteps, left the family home.

When Miranda arrived with Ben she found Pen's note on

the kitchen table. The words didn't immediately register with her. Having read them she called up the stairs for Pen to come down and explain. Then she re-read them and the fear took hold. She reached for the phone but put it down again: she was wondering whether to dial 999 or ring round some of Pen's schoolfriends when the phone rang. 'Pen?' she said frantically. Ben was tugging at her leg, wailing pitiably for a biscuit.

'Miranda, are you alright?' Anne covered the receiver and called Clive into the room. She knew an emergency when she heard one.

'No. I'm not alright.' There was the sound of a scuffle, then Ben's screaming diminishing as he ran from the room. 'Pen's gone.'

'Gone?'

'Yes. Gone. Gone!'

'Wait there. We're coming over.'

Anne signalled to Clive to fetch the keys and get the car started. Clive wandered to his jacket in the study then went outside and waited in the car. He had spent much of the last twenty-four hours convincing Anne that the regular out-goings from the business account were payments to an organised gang who'd moved onto his industrial estate and demanded protection money. Two units had already been 'torched'; two hundred quid a month was worth it for peace of mind. Anne had a blind spot where the 'underclass' was concerned which is why, Clive always reckoned, she married him. The reason he had wanted to marry her had, for a number of years, completely eluded him.

Having got the gist of the call from Miranda, Clive didn't take long to work out where Pen was going. The next few hours were going to be a test of character. There was no need to reveal Gordon's whereabouts; he would go there alone and reconstruct the chase later on.

'Drive.' The suspension dropped as Anne got into the passenger seat. They were half-way through the gate before she'd slammed the door. Beads of sweat had appeared on her upper lip and she was scanning the road ahead like a traffic cop.

When Clive and Anne arrived at Miranda's, the road looked as if it was set for a siege drama. Piran's Porsche with its hazard lights flashing, a police car spilling static from an open window and the quiet couple's Golf Cabriolet with the top down were raked at varying angles to the kerb. Miranda's front door was open.

Clive and Anne went in and followed the commotion to the kitchen. A flustered policewoman was removing gummy pieces of Marmited bread from her collar, Ben was perched on the work surface eating orange Wotsits and playing with a pair of handcuffs, Piran was jacketed but loose-tied at the sink cradling a large Scotch, and Miranda was weeping into her hands at the kitchen table as the quiet woman massaged her shoulders. Then a tall man, whom Clive recalled as Stephen from Piran's dinner party, came in, went immediately over to Miranda and kissed her full on the lips. This was too much to take in so Clive went back into the lounge and surreptitiously switched on the television news as snatches of hysteria, police waveband crackle, raised voices and ponderous appeals for calm reached him from the kitchen. Then, like a rowing boat emerging from a storm, Ben walked in with the handcuffs.

'I need a pooh, I do,' he said, glad to have found at least one adult whose attention he could command.

'Fine. Lead the way, little fellow,' Clive said.

'I'm not little,' Ben said, banging the handcuffs percussively against the banisters. He paused when they were half-way up and broke wind. 'That was you, it was,' Ben announced, then continued into the lavatory.

Clive waited outside the door as the child strained noisily inside, then he caught sight of Pen's bedroom door and it occurred to him that the police might not have searched the room yet. He went quietly in and immediately saw the map of Egypt, stiffly folded in on itself on the floor.

The scrunched note was beside the wastepaper basket. Hearing footsteps on the stairs, he slipped it into his pocket as Piran walked in.

'There you are.' Piran extended his hand in a funeral greeting.

'How is she?' Clive said, opening Pen's top drawer and rifling through it.

'Miranda? Oh, pretty much how you'd expect.'

'Yes?'

'We should have seen it coming. It's always the ones who seem to be most in control who go off the rails, isn't it?'

'Pen, you mean?'

'Yes. The little thing bottles it up. But she sees it all, you know. I'd say she was wiser than all of us.'

'I don't suppose that would be too hard would it?' Clive closed the drawer then went to the door and pushed it to. 'I know where Gordon is.'

'Yes. I imagined you might.'

'I'll go straight there. You'll have to keep busy round here. I don't want Miranda knowing. Not yet.'

'Have you known all along?'

'Yes.'

'How is he?'

'I don't know. Fit enough to cash a monthly cheque.'

'Good for him. I can't say I'd object to three months off.'

'Is that how he sees it, do you reckon?'

'I don't know. Wishful thinking on my part, I suppose.'

'I've finished!' Ben appeared from the lavatory, pushing the door open, then dropped to his hands and knees. 'Wipe my bottom.'

Clive obliged.

After they had unlocked the handcuffs which Ben had used to attach himself to the banisters, it was agreed that the police effort would be augmented by search parties led by Piran, Clive and the quiet woman. Piran would go to the M1 and watch the junctions, the quiet woman and Anne tour the railway terminals and Clive would have a roving brief. Nobody knew quite what to say about Stephen who hovered proprietorially behind Miranda as they filed past her on their way out.

'It will be alright,' Piran said, taking her hand and kissing it. Miranda nodded. Clive touched her shoulder and followed him out. The night was cold and the moon was full: swollen and white, mocking their insignificance. They all found themselves thinking of Pen as they trooped to their cars. Her disappearance had touched them to a degree few of them would have believed themselves capable of feeling. All would have traded everything they had just to bring the child back home.

The cars filed from the street. Clive drove off last. He switched on the car stereo and prepared himself for the long drive north.

EIGHT

Pen was eating her sandwiches on the train. She had bought a chilled triangular plastic box of cheese and tomato at the station buffet. She had wanted a packet of cheese and onion crisps but the man at the counter had flustered her into a hurried purchase. She felt sorry for herself and was beginning to question what she was doing, chasing half-way up the country after her father who probably didn't want to see her anyway. An old woman in the seat opposite kept clucking like a hen and trying to catch her eye. Pen ignored her until the woman could bear it no longer and asked her directly just where she was going, at this time of night, on her own. Pen named the station she was heading for but offered no other details. The old woman went back to her crossword puzzle book, and Pen slipped the head-phones of her Walkman over her ears, shutting out the sound of the carriage.

After leaving the house she had gone round to the Monnerys'. Somehow she felt that Connie would be able to help her even if it was only to the extent of assuring her that she was doing the right thing. But Connie had hung on the doorframe and not invited her in. It was almost as though they'd never met. Connie could have sent her home, but she didn't, she encouraged her to go. It was something she'd been intending to do for ages and not quite got round to. Pen left, feeling a little less for Connie than she had before.

The world was complex and unpredictable but Pen had always been able to see things clearly. Where her friends vacillated, Pen always knew what she thought. Her moral codes were finely developed; if anyone transgressed her rules then she froze them out. As a result, she had few close friends, but couldn't find it in her heart to care, even though she considered she had every right to feel angry. What made her most angry were people who stood in her way. Because she knew what was right and what was not, she couldn't bear to be told that she was wrong.

Sometimes her teachers treated her like a child and she hadn't felt like a child for almost as long as she could remember. Her father didn't treat her like a child. He seemed almost afraid of her. When he came into the room, she often found herself feeling sorry for him. It was as if he didn't quite know what to say. She wouldn't have minded if they didn't speak for a year. She knew that, deep down, he cared for her, and that was all that really mattered. She was going to find him and bring him back, as much for his sake as hers. Her parents needed her help. Pen fingered the small blue ticket she had found in the bottom of her father's envelope. She would ask him what it meant, if she ever found him.

When the train stopped and the old lady got off, a man in a blue suit took her place. Pen was aware of him watching her so she looked away and stared out of the window. There was something about him she didn't like. He reminded her of the man in the newsagent's who always came from behind the counter and stood too close when she was looking for a magazine. When his wife was there it was different, he didn't bother.

'There you are, Mr Meadows.' Mrs Hill was lying on the sofa in a thin blue dressing gown which showed an ample area of her bust and a significant expanse of thigh. Gordon waited by the door. It had never occurred to him that Mrs Hill had ever felt anything for him sexually. He had always assumed that looking after her mother accounted for her entire emotional output.

'I hope you don't mind the informality?' Her voice was softer than usual, as if, having shed her carer's uniform, she had lost a little of the harshness that the role required.

'Of course not.'

'Then come in and help yourself to a sherry.' A small bar had been built into the corner of the room. It had been fashioned to resemble a boat's prow with a high stool on both the port and starboard sides. The glass shelves behind were full of cheerfully bright liqueurs and the bar itself was lit by two seashell-encrusted lamps. Gordon examined the stock for recognisable brand names but came swiftly to the conclusion that a sweet sherry was probably the safest bet.

'Top me up, will you?' Mrs Hill waved her large schooner in the air. Gordon took it from her hot hand. Her look fixed on him as their fingers briefly touched but Gordon quickly turned away. When he carried the two drinks over, Mrs Hill had swung her legs back in front of her, arranged her dressing gown to cover herself more effectively and adopted her characteristic look of scepticism. He sat down beside her and they sipped in silence.

'I imagined, you see, that you'd stay,' Mrs Hill said, continuing the thought from the previous morning.

'Yes. It did seem to come as a surprise to you.'

'It was a shock. I won't deny it. You see I always pride myself on being a good judge of character. The Polish gentleman excepted. A few others. Men, of course.'

'I can't see you being taken in by anybody, Mrs Hill.'

'Well, you see a woman who's had her fair share of heartbreak. I'm sure, seeing me with Mother every day, you probably think I've never lived. But I have lived. I have.' She contemplated the fire over the rim of her sherry glass, breathing in the fumes.

'You never married?'

'No I didn't. I never found a man I could spend a lifetime with. I don't believe men have it in them for a lifetime's commitment.'

'Don't you?'

'I don't. I lost my virginity to a piano tuner. You don't mind me talking like this?'

'Of course not.' Gordon relaxed a little on the sofa.

'Mother had him here twice a year, though nobody touched the instrument from one year to the next. It was a whim of my father's. He left before I was old enough to know him.'

'I'm sorry.'

'No. I have no regrets. My mother more than made up for him. But I do remember his piano playing. I think I must have heard it from my cot. But I remember it. I suppose mother was keeping it tuned for him, for if he ever came back. The tuner seduced me; though, his being blind, I have to take part of the blame. Fine, sensitive hands he had. But a sad man. A wistful man. I've always judged other men by what I learned from him. Perhaps he was too kind.'

'And how do you judge me?'

'Well. There's a thing, you see. I don't have you marked down as dangerous. Not like, well, Mr Blake, say.'

'Blake?'

'Oh yes. All that neatness ... I'd never entirely trust a fastidious man. I think I'd always find myself questioning what he was hiding. But then I don't imagine you've ever been privy to the contents of Mr Blake's wastepaper basket.'

'No. I don't think I have.'

'He folds his tissues, Mr Meadows. There's a man on the edge if ever I saw one . . . Of course, there was the business with the child. But that wasn't his fault.'

'Yes, but you were saying . . .' Gordon was greedy only for insights into his own condition.

'You . . . well, I'd have to give the matter some thought.' Gordon allowed her to think. 'I think I'd be forced to admit to seeing a rather selfish man.'

'Would you?'

'We all spend time . . . looking inwards. Perhaps not Mr Blake who needs to concentrate on what's going on all around him. But for the rest of us I suppose we're happy with what we find. I'd say you'd feel differently.'

'I ran away from home,' Gordon blurted. 'And I don't really know why. Except that I could no longer live the life I was leading.'

'Yes. I once had a commercial traveller who was similarly afflicted. He used to stay for a night every now and again. He regularly complained of being trapped. We often spoke about it over cocktails in this very room.'

'And what happened to him?'

'Oh, he left home. I think he had a small boy. But he was soon trapped somewhere else. We carry our cages with us, Gordon.'

Gordon found the use of his name peculiarly erotic. Mrs Hill had let her dressing gown ride a little higher. She had good legs. Perhaps it was the sherry, but Gordon was beginning to feel a strange pull towards the woman.

'What do you think I should do?'

'Well . . . I suppose I should say you should go back to your family. You do have a family, I expect?'

'Yes.'

'If that's what you feel. You must do as you feel right.'

'That's the thing, you see,' Gordon said enthusiastically, 'I think I've stopped knowing what I feel. I know what I'm expected to feel, I know what feelings are, but I can't, somehow, feel them.'

'I see.'

'Does that make sense?'

'Yes, I can see that. I can quite see that. But that leaves you in rather a pickle, doesn't it?'

'I suppose it does.'

'I mean, perhaps you need something to take your mind away. You see?' Mrs Hill's hand went to Gordon's thigh. He shuffled away but she clung on. 'Sometimes you can spend too much time thinking about yourself without really seeing what's going on in front of your eyes.'

Despite an urge to stay and give Mrs Hill whatever small encouragements she needed to continue, Gordon struggled out of the chair. 'I think,' he said formally, 'I'd better get to bed.'

'If you like, Gordon.' Mrs Hill reached for the television remote and switched channels. 'Only you wouldn't have had any complaints. The commercial traveller said he'd never had a better time.'

'I'm sure. It's not you . . . it's just.'

'We'd lie almost naked in front of the open fire. I've never felt any guilt in that department, you see.'

Miranda put Ben to bed while Stephen cleared up the house. The police telephoned at eight o'clock but there was nothing to report. Miranda would have preferred the phone not to ring. She had a superstition that there would be only so many calls before there was a knock on the door. They would come with the bad news to the house; if the news was good then they would call. She allowed herself two more calls. Two more and then . . . then the unimaginable. It was too big to contemplate; no words she could find came anywhere near to defining it.

Stephen waited in the silent living room holding a glass of wine. The television was off, the curtains were undrawn. Across the street, the far terrace was closing itself up for the night. Miranda stood watching as the windows darkened like eyes closing tight.

'Can I get you anything?' Stephen said.

'I'll tell you if you can. Please don't keep asking.'

'I'm sorry.'

'Is this our fault?'

'What?' Stephen joined Miranda at the window.

'Our, my, payment for us. For what happened between us.'

'Of course it isn't.'

'I'm not so sure. I've never been able to trust feeling good; it's a curse. I used to think everybody felt like me. Apparently they don't.'

'No.'

'I used to think – why? Why am I feeling good, why am I being allowed to feel good? What's just around the corner waiting to come and take it away. Then, of course, as soon as I felt like that all the goodness was gone. Do you feel like that?'

'No. I was raised to believe . . .' Stephen wrapped his arm carefully around Miranda's shoulder. She reached across her breast to take his hand in hers.

'Go on.'

'. . . I think my mother wanted me to have everything. Particularly happiness. I suppose I was spoilt by her. At least that was what my father always said. I tended to believe him more than her. I needed him to approve of me. He never did. Her approval wasn't worth having.'

'But she loved you?'

'Like any mother loves a son. Too much, but not enough to teach me about women. I suppose she thought I'd find somebody like her. To love me in the way she did. Of course that's an impossible burden to put on anyone. You're the first woman I've loved who's had a child.'

'Loved?'

'Yes.'

'Does it come that easily to you?'

'Oh yes. Always.'

Miranda said, 'Perhaps if I'd lived with someone like you it would have been different.'

'Yes.'

'Except I honestly don't think it would.'

The phone rang. Miranda ran into the kitchen.

'Miranda . . .' It was Piran calling from the car. The road washed by in the background. 'I thought I'd check in, see if there was . . .' The voice broke up. '. . . to report.'

'Nothing. Where are you?' Miranda sensed Stephen come into the kitchen behind her.

'I'm . . . just past junction sixteen. On the M1.'

'I thought you were . . .'

'Clive phoned. I'm just following instructions.'

'Call me.'

'Yes. Take care.'

Miranda put the phone down. Another call. Just one to go.

'He said "take care". I wonder what he wanted to say.' Stephen said. 'I don't suppose he really knows.'

Miranda heard footsteps on the stairs, then a break, then fast padding along the hallway and into the kitchen.

Ben waited and watched Stephen warily. Stephen backed away and out into the lounge. Miranda picked Ben up and smothered her face in his warm hair.

The world was different at night. As she got off the train Pen realised that she'd never been out alone this late before. She didn't much like it. People were different. They looked different. Everybody seemed to be watching her and each other, like the man in the blue suit. It was as though they were expecting something more of each other than they did in the day. But perhaps it was just her imagination. The carriages slid away up the platform: aquariums of light; white, disinterested faces. Pen walked across the bridge and down into the ticket hall which was cheerfully and commercially bright after the sinister shadows of the northbound platform. A paper stall was taking delivery of bundles of magazines. A fat man sweated as he cut the ties around each bundle with a sharp knife.

Pen had nearly ten pounds left in her purse which she hoped would get her to the park where the ticket in her father's envelope had come from. That was as far as she knew. When she got there she'd trust her instincts to get her further. She stopped at the buffet and bought a Mars bar. As soon as she got out of the station she unwrapped it but it didn't taste right. Her stomach felt strange. It was tight, as though there was a huge heavy ball on top of it and she was having to keep it up. It made her breathe more heavily and feel a different kind of sadness from the sadness she usually felt.

She walked up to a taxi and waited by the door. She didn't know whether to get straight in or whether she had to wait to be asked. Being grown up was a simple matter of learning the answers to questions such as these. The tired man in the cap was reading an evening paper propped on the steering wheel and eating a sandwich. His thin white elbow was poking through the open window. Pen coughed. He looked up at her then behind her looking for a parent.

'Will you take me to this park?' Pen proffered the small

blue ticket to the man. He took it and pushed his glasses back onto his forehead to scrutinise it more closely. 'I'm meeting my father,' Pen said, anticipating his next question.

'Bit late isn't it, pet?'

'He works in the park.' She waited. The man reached behind him and flung open the back door. Pen sat in the back seat with her bag on her lap. She felt quite grown up as they swept out from the station and onto the ring road.

Mrs Hill knocked on Gordon's bedroom door and came in when he called. She was dressed again. The formality had returned. 'Mr Blake is not in his room.'

'Isn't he?'

Mrs Hill went to the window and looked at the moon. 'I'd go and look for him only I can't leave Mother.'

'So you want . . . I see. So you want me to go and find him?'

'I think that would be for the best, wouldn't it, Mr Meadows?' Unspoken was the accusation that Gordon's night out had, in some way, disrupted Blake's routine to the extent that he was now in some kind of danger.

'Alright, just give me a moment.' Gordon began clearing the papers from his bed. He'd been trying to sort through what he'd accumulated over the past three months. The pile of papers he was not intending to discard was pitifully thin. Whether that represented the success or failure of his time away was unclear to him.

'He's a good man at the heart of it all. Remember that.'

'I know he is. I've always had a soft spot for Mr Blake.'

'That business with the child. It wasn't his fault.'

'I'm sorry?'

'There was some business about a young boy. Mr Blake claims he was only trying to teach the boy to read. You see?'

'Right.'

'Only when he loses his . . . balance, sometimes I think he goes through it all again.' Mrs Hill was uncomfortable with imparting the details; she had hoped that Gordon would get the picture more quickly so she wouldn't have to explain.

'How do you mean?'

'They found him. Some parents. There was an ugly scene. Mr Blake fled for his life, but they caught him. The mind . . . it plays tricks on us all, doesn't it?'

Piran's car phone rang.

'Clive's found Gordon. He asked me to give you the address.' It was Miranda.

'Christ. Where?'

'He's tracked him down to some lodging house. I assume he knew he was there all along, but I don't have time to get angry about that now. He's gone out looking for someone. Which is absolutely typical of him.'

'Don't worry, just tell me where they are. Give me a number I can call Clive on.'

Clive was sitting in the kitchen with Mrs Hill when the phone rang. Mrs Hill was pouring him a cup of tea and talking about a man called Blake. It was clear she was worried about him, and when Clive explained about Pen, she nearly dropped the teapot.

'Are you Clive?' Mrs Hill called him to the phone in the hallway. The stair banisters were white and made from swirls of thin metal. The carpet was a shock of orange spirals. Clive watched Mrs Hill wiping the kitchen table with a dishcloth as he spoke to Piran. Soon she was back at the phone, giving Piran directions to a park which seemed to be quite close to her house. She repeated them when she rang off and Clive went in search of Gordon.

When it happened, it seemed to happen quite quickly. But from the time Gordon reached the park to the time the ambulance arrived was almost an hour. After leaving the house, Gordon had first checked the shopping precinct but it was empty except for three girls leaning against the fish and chip shop window and sharing a can of Diet Pepsi. They hadn't seen a large man but as all three of them thought Gordon was just trying to pick them up they didn't give the matter any serious consideration. It was then that Gordon realised the last time he'd seen Blake was at the park, so he jogged down the hill and covered the half mile in a creditable time.

He slowed when he reached the lavatories on the edge of the play area. Two cars were parked on the hard shoulder beside them. He saw the blur of a head through the ground glass of the window. When he went in, a cubicle door was slammed shut. He looked under the door and saw two sets of legs. Neither of them were Blake's so he walked out, past the gate that had fallen from its hinges and along the edge of the outer lake which was used on Sundays by strange men with radio-controlled boats.

The park was shaped like a figure eight. Gordon passed through the narrow waist of it, squeezed by the fields that encroached at each side, then he came out beside the lake. The moonlight lit his way. The bare trees on the island were cloaked in silver. He stopped beside his hut and peered carefully around the perimeter of the lake. Nothing. He squinted towards the island and saw a rowing boat, half hauled from the lake. A voice reached him across the flat, silent water. But it wasn't Blake's voice. It was the voice of a child. An odd sing-song. High and happy, or tearful.

At that moment he heard a roar from the far side of the park and saw two headlights bouncing across the uneven earth of the football pitches. As the car came closer he recognised it as the type he'd always coveted. His friend, Piran, used to have one. Perhaps he still did. The headlights were coming towards him now. The car accelerated over the rough ground. It skidded to a stop and Piran got out.

'Have you seen her?' Piran said, he was gaunt, afraid. Something had happened.

'What?' It was Piran but because of the absurdity of encountering him here, Gordon's mind was busy computing the odds of encountering someone who looked remarkably like him and also drove the same type of car.

'Pen's gone missing and come looking for you, Gordon. Have you seen her?'

'Pen?' Gordon's mouth opened again but nothing came out. The conversation with Mrs Hill about Blake suddenly made more sense, though at the time she surely couldn't have known about his daughter. With the absurd logic of a nightmare another man arrived. It was Clive, bobbing like a boxer, looking at him and Piran, trying to work out for himself was what was going on. Then Clive put a reassuring arm on his when Gordon felt it should have been the other way round.

'Over there. I think she's over there.' Gordon pointed at the boat on the island, at the same time tugging off his coat and kicking off his shoes. 'With Blake. Christ, she must be with Blake.'

Piran dropped his jacket onto the grass, Clive unclipped his watch, but Gordon was already in the water, half-wading, stumbling, swimming through the dense weeds. As they watched, he bobbed completely out of sight, then he was back up again shaking the water from his eyes. Clive plunged in after him and was a third of the way across when Gordon reached the island and set off into the trees, the water falling from him like broken glass.

Clive was almost there when he heard a shout. It was

barely human. He waded towards it then two figures stumbled from the trees, one tugging the other. Blake was in a head-lock, Gordon was hauling him towards the water, smashing his right fist into the large man's face again and again. Blake was screaming in pain and fear, his arms were waving as though he was trying to swim through the air.

Gordon hauled him upright. Blake reached for his face and blinked the blood from his eyes. He looked like a bull in a slaughterhouse. Gordon pushed him hard down the short bank. Blake tripped over his feet and fell the final distance on his knees. When he hit the water he went under, face first. Then his broad shoulders came up and he tried to stand; a bubble of air was caught beneath his coat.

Gordon scanned the trees frantically looking for Pen. He saw the white flash of a face coming from the centre of the island; a small figure walking slowly towards him. Behind him Blake went down again, and Clive waded after him to help him out. Gordon ran into the trees, towards the white face. He called for his daughter and a child called back. Then Pen walked into the clearing, composed, her clothes not dishevelled. She saw her father but looked away towards the water. Blake was standing now, his face resigned, no longer afraid, just another punishment meted out to him for a reason he did not fully understand by a world he never wanted to be a part of.

'Pen . . . ?' Gordon said, and waited for her to run to him. Instead, she took a handkerchief from her bag and slipped off her shoes. She waded carefully into the lake, pushed Clive aside, then knelt in the icy water and put her arm round Blake's shoulders. He winced at the contact, then, seeing it was her, let her cradle his head in her arms.

'He didn't hurt me,' she called across the water to Gordon. 'Not like you.'

The enormity of his desertion fell on Gordon's shoulders.

'We were waiting for you to come. I asked him to take me onto the island. He didn't want to steal a boat.'

Blake's head was bowed, his jaw hung open. The top set of his false teeth fell from his mouth. A silver string of spittle seemed to suspend them, then they fell into the water.

Gordon looked at Blake, knowing that it couldn't have been he who had delivered the punishment. He was incapable of such violence. Violence suggested a depth of passion beyond his limited repertoire. With Pen's help, Blake climbed onto the bank and sat there panting.

PART THREE

ONE

'WHAT ARE YOU doing for Christmas?'
'Not sure,' Gordon said reflexively, looking up
from his newspaper to see Monnery standing with his hands
in his pockets and gaping across the room towards the door.
The teaching practice girl was bending over a small rucksack
and pulling out a wad of orange exercise books. The dull
morning was being kept at bay by the sterile brightness of the
staff room's fluorescent lights.

'Mm.' Monnery slumped down beside him. 'I suppose
you know when you're getting old. It's not the policemen
who start looking younger, it's kids you taught coming back
to school to join the staff. Thank you very much Sandra
Vickers.'

Sandra Vickers caught sight of Monnery as she went out of
the room. She waved and Monnery blushed and looked
away.

'You could come to us on Christmas Day. We're going on
a duty tour to the Olds on Boxing Day. Jan said you'd be
welcome.'

'Thanks.'

'Bring a bottle. Nothing formal. It'll just be the two of us.
Connie will no doubt be out with the spotty oik's family,

135

Belinda and Geoff, social workers. We never see her now, you know.'

'I think we're going to Hampshire.'

'We?'

'Me and Sandra Vickers.'

'You're not!'

Gordon folded his newspaper and slid it into the sodden residue at the bottom of the grey wastepaper bin. 'Of course I'm not. Piran's invited us all down to Pop's old place. Sort of farewell to it before he sells it. His mother's already been shipped out to Greece. Miranda thinks we should go as a family.'

'What about whatsisname?'

'Oh, he'll be there. When Miranda talks about "family", you see, she tends to include him ahead of me.'

'Mm.' Monnery was looking boredly round the room for another female to fix his attentions on. 'I suppose this freedom thing does have a lot going for it. You know, swinging singles, that sort of thing.'

'Singles don't swing. They sag. At least the one I met did.'

'You've been out with one?'

'Well, not really. Sandy introduced me to one. She was fifty-odd and built like an all-in wrestler. She told me afterwards she'd met her at some Women's Group. I was lectured for an hour about the transportation of live animals, then she grabbed me by the balls and asked me how I'd feel if I was chained all day up by my knackers.'

'Sandy must be due soon, I expect.'

'January.'

'Sticky one, isn't it?'

'Not really.'

'Well it is, I mean, what if it comes out looking like you?'

'It won't. It's not mine. My sperm gave up the ghost years ago.'

'Jan said that Miranda was saying . . .'

'Monnery. Shut up.'

Monnery retrieved Gordon's paper from the bin and unfolded it onto his lap. A tea bag had already bled cold tannin across the headlines. 'I just thought you might be interested in Miranda's current thinking on the situation.'

'I know what she thinks. And I can't say I blame her.'

'I don't think it's at all black and white.'

'It never is when Jan gets hold of something.'

Monnery ruminated on the accuracy of Gordon's observation, then he offered a token, 'I think that's a bit unfair, isn't it?'

'Is it?' Gordon had buried his face in his hands and was massaging his cheeks to try and get rid of the numbness in them. The palms of his hands smelt of carbolic. That morning, he'd nicked himself shaving and hadn't even felt it. Since he'd been back he'd felt a dislocation from the life going on around him. The sharper, most acute feelings of loss were the ones that got through, but they were the ones he didn't want to feel. Nothing good ever seemed to come along to relieve them. He was in what Monnery had called 'a no-win situation', although he didn't regret for a moment coming back: at least now he could begin to face the reasons that prompted him to leave. If only he could discover what those reasons were.

'You really screwed it up, didn't you?' Monnery lobbed another log on the fire of his misery. He seemed to be enjoying Gordon's dilemma; at least it allowed him to forget his own for a while.

'Yes.' Gordon sighed. 'Yes, I did.'

'How's Pen?'

'Fine. I think. We're going out tonight so she can let me spend some money on her. She worked out quite fast that

137

the size of her wardrobe and my guilt have some inextricable link.'

'I'm glad she's alright.'

'So am I.'

'And Ben?'

'Who knows.'

When Gordon called round at the place he still called home, Stephen answered the door. The two men were working hard at being civilised with each other so the greeting between them was more effusive than either of them felt. Stephen pumped Gordon's hand all the way from the front door to the kitchen where Pen was finishing her homework. Gordon agreed to stay and have a drink until Pen was ready. He felt an urgent need to hit Stephen when he saw him going to his drinks cabinet, move aside his decent bottle of single malt, and pull out the cheap emergency bottle of supermarket blend.

'I must come and collect some of that stuff,' Gordon said as he took the glass. 'I collect whiskies. Bit of a habit I got in to.'

'Sure. Talk to Miranda.' Stephen unscrewed the cap from a blue bottle of fizzy water and poured it carefully into a thick-bottomed glass. The expensive glassware was one of the many changes Gordon had noticed around the house. The settees looked as though they'd been re-covered, but it seemed they'd been cleaned. The grey carpet had been replaced by something Miranda said was made of some sort of grass; there was a huge bowl of enormous tropical flowers in the window, and the room had been painted in a shocking primary blue which gave Gordon a claustrophobic headache whenever he walked in. The crowning glory, and most painful symbol of his plight, was a huge oil painting of a naked woman on the wall opposite the fire. The woman looked remarkably similar to Miranda, but her figure was noticeably thinner and her pubic hair was missing. Miranda had undoubtedly lost weight since he'd been away, but Gordon couldn't bring himself to question her about the veracity of the rendering in the downstairs department.

When Gordon was away it had felt like less than a week. Now he was back the time seemed to have stretched into years. There was no place for him at home any more. Even Pen, whom he'd always considered to be an ally, was now mentioning Stephen regularly and without her customary condescension. Miranda was acting cool. He knew her well enough to know that she was rather surprised that Stephen was still around, having, by now, been given the unexpurgated version of his wife – and yet he still doted on her. He was always touching her, petting her, snatching kisses when he could, and while all these displays of affection were ones she'd always accused Gordon of never showing, she seemed slightly uncomfortable with it. He also observed that Stephen needed regular reassurances of the strength of their relationship. He had a tendency to storm around when he felt he wasn't getting the attention he deserved. There was something brittle about the man that his patrician disdain failed to mask.

Stephen hadn't moved in. This they often reiterated to Gordon. But he did seem to be there whenever Gordon went round. Miranda had, however, invited Gordon out for a meal on their wedding anniversary. She reassured him it wasn't a joke, it just seemed that they never spent time together and they needed to talk about the future and the children, and whatever was to happen next. This was set for Tuesday the following week, and Gordon was still wondering whether in the circumstances an anniversary card was appropriate.

'Have you thought about Christmas?' Stephen said,

making it immediately clear that he would prefer it if Gordon stayed away.

'Yes. I think I should come, don't you?'

'Of course. If that is what you want.'

'I'll come down with you. Share the driving if you like.'

'I don't imagine there will be room. It's only Hampshire, anyway.'

'I'll take Pen then. Or Ben. I don't mind.'

'Yes. Speak to Miranda.'

'I will.'

Gordon's glass was already empty. He wanted to go now. The blue of the walls was crowding in on him like a high sea. Each time he came home it was harder to stay but the alternative was his small flat with the tiny kitchenette, the balding purple bedspread, the malfunctioning shower; a cold place devoid of comfort.

Gordon heard the front door slam and the urgent scuff of feet along the corridor. Ben scampered into the room in a red duffel coat buttoned almost to his nose. He was holding a small metal aeroplane. He brummed it around, stopped by Stephen and said, 'I'm going to dead you.' He was manic with the joy of life, his cheeks were already red from the heat of the room.

Gordon waited for Stephen to laugh, but he didn't. Instead, he snatched the toy from Ben's hand and put it on the mantelpiece. 'We don't say that, do we, Ben?' Ben scowled and tried to cross his eyes. He looked at Gordon as he would a stranger and ran out of the room. Gordon went to the fireplace and picked up the tiny plane.

Stephen said, 'We're not keen on aggression.'

'I don't think that was aggression, was it?'

'Ben needs to know what his boundaries are.'

'I'm sure he does. But if you set them too narrow he'll always be running into them.'

'I think we need to be consistent. There's no point in him having one set of rules here, and another with you.'

'I couldn't agree more.' Gordon weighed the die-cast model in his hand then put it down again as Miranda came in. Stephen leaped up and intercepted her before she'd got half-way across the room. Gordon knew she had been heading over to kiss him but by the time Stephen had squeezed the life out of her, all she could manage was a quick pinch of his hand. She was blushing.

'Where's Ben?' she asked Stephen.

'He ran off. I had to take his plane away. He said he was going to dead me.'

'Did he hit you with it?'

'No.'

Miranda was about to say something else, then she seemed suddenly to be aware of Gordon's intense interest in the exchange and sat down in a neutral chair. She breathed hard and managed a smile.

'So . . .' she said. 'How are you?'

'Bloody awful, really,' Gordon said.

'What about the flat. Are you settled?'

'I must borrow some sheets.'

'Yes. I'll look some out for you . . . How about school?'

'Oh, fine. Nothing changes.'

Miranda's mask slipped. 'But then that's up to you, isn't it? To make it change, I mean.'

'It's all I know. If I could stop doing it then I would. I don't know how to do anything else.' It struck Gordon that one of the markers of his existence was the belief that somebody would actually care if that existence ceased. At that moment he could think of nobody beyond Pen who would.

'. . . So . . .' Stephen said for Miranda's sake, to fill the extensive pause that followed.

'Look, I'd better get off,' Gordon said. 'Has Pen finished?'

'Pen!' Stephen called. 'Have you finished? Gordon wants to go.'

'Nearly.'

'. . . I thought I'd come down with you at Christmas.' Gordon ushered the remark towards Miranda, taking the final opportunity for a stab at Stephen.

'Oh.'

'Is that a problem?'

'No. It's just that Jan called and said you were going round there.'

'Well I'm not. Monnery asked me today but I told him I was coming down with you. I think I did, anyway.'

'I'll have to call Sandy then, see if she can fix up another room.'

'I thought you wanted me to come.'

'I do. Of course we do. But she called today and I told her . . . look, it's no problem.'

'Or perhaps you'd rather I spent Christmas on my own?'

'I'd rather you did what you wanted to do, Gordon, like you always do.'

'Oh, come on.'

'I mean, I'm sure Mrs Hill or whatever her name is could put you up for a few nights.'

Stephen looked on patiently. To Gordon's surprise he didn't seem to be enjoying the exchange.

'Pen!' Gordon called, and Pen immediately responded to the urgency in his voice by appearing at the door with her coat across her arm.

'Finished,' she said.

'Right.' Gordon looked into the kitchen for Ben but he was upstairs. 'Bye, Ben!' he called.

After a loud thud, Ben appeared round the top of the stairs tugging his huge quilt behind him. He had a small corner of

it clenched in his right fist and was sucking his thumb.
'Goodbye, darling,' Gordon said.

'Bye bye,' Ben said with an unconjured sadness.

Gordon leaped up the stairs two at a time and pulled Ben
into his arms. When Miranda called to ask if everything was
alright he went into the bathroom and splashed water on his
face. He didn't want either of them to see him crying.

Pen wasn't really hungry. She didn't particularly want to go
out, but she knew her father wanted to see her so she did her
best with him. When he asked about her day she even
managed to find one or two things that interested him. They
walked clockwise round the park but this only took ten
minutes.

'I suppose you could take me to the pub,' Pen said.

'You don't want to go to the pub, do you? Anyway, we'd
have to sit outside and it's freezing.'

'I could have some crisps.' The offer saved face on both
sides so they went to the pub with the tables outside and sat
together in the winter cold. The embers of the day burnt as
coals of red cloud in the black sky.

'I've been writing to Mr Blake,' Pen said.

'Blake?'

'You know.'

'Oh, Blake.' Gordon's mind flashed to the lake and the
dentures fished out and handed to the broken man.

'He's in a hospital, but he says he's getting better. He sent
me a drawing of a budgie. I thought I might ask Mummy if
he can come and stay.'

'I don't think so.'

'Why not?'

'Well . . . well, he's. I mean. Well, she doesn't even know
him.'

'No. But I do. And you do. And I think we should do things for people like that.'

'Yes, but there's doing things and doing things, isn't there.'

'What do you mean?'

'I mean it's like giving money to charity, you can't give everything you have away, so you have to choose.'

'Yes, but it's not money, it's having him down here. That's the only choice.'

'. . . I suppose you'd better ask Mummy.'

'If she says he can't stay with us, will you let him stay with you?'

'. . . I suppose so . . . yes, why not.'

'Thank you, Daddy.' Pen smiled warmly.

'How are you getting on with Stephen?' Gordon tried.

'Alright. I don't mind him. Sometimes he's cross with Ben.' Pen seemed to want to say more but she stopped herself and took a drink of her Coke. 'Do you think you'll be coming back home?'

'I don't know, Pen.'

'Do you want to?'

'Of course I do. But I can hardly come back with Stephen there, can I?'

'Oh, he doesn't matter. Not really . . . I'm glad you want to come back. Because then you will.' Pen smiled again. Everything was settled in her mind. She'd brought her father back, now all she had to do was to get him to move back in.

Gordon had arranged to meet Miranda at the pub the following Tuesday; he couldn't face the prospect of another encounter with Stephen. He'd tried to call Sandy, but Piran had answered the phone and he was too embarrassed to ask to speak to her. The friends had been distant with him since he got back. On the first Saturday of the month he had expected to be called round to Piran and Sandy's for supper but the call never came. He knew they'd met because he spoke to Clive the following day to check. Miranda had, of course, gone with Stephen, and while it was clear that Stephen was not widely liked, the interloper was nevertheless now more part of the circle than he was. Gordon just didn't fit in any more and he knew Sandy had not expected him to take up the Christmas invitation.

While he had no right to be hurt or angry, he was. Surely, he argued with Clive, they knew he wasn't going to cause a scene. And anyway, he and Stephen got on well enough. But that wasn't the issue. The point was that he'd slept with Sandy. The fact that Clive had done the same obviously wasn't relevant because Clive had never been found out. So Gordon's new social life consisted of picking off his friends one by one, usually when they were on their way somewhere else. These evenings had a tendency always to begin with 'sorry, can't stay long, I'm going . . . ' wherever. One evening Gordon was so bored he went to a pub close to the school where he knew some of the sixth formers met. He stood a couple of rounds but left when he realised they weren't at all interested in what he had to say, they were spurring him on simply to take the rise out of him.

He had met Sandy the week he came back. She phoned him at school and when he returned the call he felt for a short while as if everything was going to be alright. They arranged to meet in the usual pub but Sandy was half an hour late so they only had a quarter of an hour together. She looked as well as he'd ever seen her looking, and the sharp irritability which had become so much a part of her over the last few years was gone. She looked almost happy, though the circles under her eyes seemed to suggest that something was nagging her.

Sandy opened with 'You've shrunk' after Gordon had manoeuvred around her pregnant stomach to kiss her.

'Only compared to you.' Gordon fetched over a proper chair for her to sit on.

'No. You look like one of those prisoners from the Japanese camps. You know, all sort of . . . I don't know . . .' Her finger drew his outline in the air, '. . . like they have a sort of shadow round them where their bodies used to come to.'

'I've not lost that much weight.'

'Perhaps it's the ghastly pallor then.'

'Thanks very much.'

'Well you wouldn't want me to lie, would you?'

'I'd rather you didn't say anything that didn't include at least some flattery.'

It seemed that Sandy had read something into what Gordon had just said. She took a moment to look more closely at him. 'Has it been terrible?'

'Yes,' Gordon said without hesitation. 'Worse since I got back, but nowhere near as bad as what Miranda's been through. I don't feel sick all the time though. I suppose that's something.'

'I'm not talking about Miranda. I'm talking about you.'

'Well the fact is, when I got back, it hardly seemed a minute since I'd gone away. But the longer I stay, the longer it seems and the less I can remember why I went in the first place. If that makes any sense.'

'You went because Piran hit you.'

'No. I went because I slept with you.'

'Alright,' said Sandy, surprised, and a little amused. 'If you're going to be direct.'

'But it wasn't just that.'

'No?'

'I wish it was. At least then . . . oh, I don't know, I'm just

146

tired of myself I suppose. I want a holiday from this miserable specimen I've been handcuffed to. I'm sure people are avoiding me because I'm such a bloody misery.'

'You've always been a misery.'

'Thanks.'

'I didn't mean it that way. I mean being miserable has always been a part of you. Some people are bright, some people are self-pitying, but you're miserable.'

'Mm.'

'Except it's not real misery, because if it was you'd try and hide it. Like Anne. I mean you can almost touch the gloom round her but she tries to cover it up with all that busybodying. Does that make sense?'

'I think so. I'm not sure it helps, though.'

They spent a little longer talking about Anne and Clive, then Sandy seemed suddenly to lose interest in the conversation.

'I've been in therapy,' she said in the next available silence, as though this was what she'd been leading up to all along. 'I just wanted to tell you. I haven't told anyone else.' Gordon felt there was a certain pride in the way she revealed the fact. Almost as if she'd taken up something like oil painting and discovered she had a real talent for it. 'I don't think Piran would understand.'

'No. I can see that.'

'I needed to sort myself out. With the baby and everything.'

Gordon waited, he didn't want to ask the next question but Sandy answered it anyway. 'It is yours, you know.'

'What?'

'You know what I'm talking about. I decided very early on to enjoy this child. And you're not going to spoil it for me.'

'How can you possibly know it's mine?'

'I knew the night it happened, well, certainly within a few days. Piran didn't come near me for weeks. Not until we went on holiday. Then I made bloody sure he did. It's going to be early. In about four weeks, I'd say. Just after Christmas.'

Gordon looked at his watch to check the date and saw that he was due in the classroom in seven minutes' time.

'So,' Sandy picked up her bag. 'Now you know.'

'Wait a minute.'

'What?'

'You can't drop something like that and just leave. Please stay for a minute.'

'I'm sorry, Gordon, I have to go. I have to spread my legs for a good-looking doctor.'

'Well, when can we talk?'

'Talk?'

'Yes, talk. There are things we need to discuss.'

'What?'

'Well . . .'

'There aren't. All you need to know is that as far as everybody's concerned the child is Piran's. That's all there is to it.'

'Of course it isn't. Jesus . . .' Gordon's look was an appeal to the disinterested audience of fellow drinkers. Surely somebody could appreciate his point of view.

'It is. Don't complicate it. There's no better way. Believe me, I've thought of little else for the past eight months.'

'And how am I supposed to feel?'

'I think you're the only one who can answer that.'

'Well why tell me? I mean if you're going ahead with this charade, why mention it at all?'

'Because you're the only person I've never lied to. I need you to be strong for me. I can't carry the lie alone. That's why.'

'I still maintain . . .' He cast around for something to keep Sandy with him. He didn't want to be alone.

'What? What do you maintain?'

'I still maintain that you can't be sure it's mine. You didn't break up with Clive until the day after, you know . . .'

'Don't be so pathetic.'

'I'm not being pathetic. I know pathetic, and in this case . . .'

'Look. Clive and I were careful. We used contraception. Always. Right? So that's why I know it's yours.'

'So why didn't we?'

'Because once, just once in our lives we were careless. And even though we've been paying for it ever since I don't regret it. Not for a moment. Alright?'

TWO

WHEN MIRANDA WALKED into the pub the following Tuesday Gordon understood for the first time what it meant to be rendered speechless. She was wearing a short petrol-blue dress he remembered having seen once before. It seemed to be advertising the fact that she had indeed lost weight. She'd also done something to her hair which had made it look brighter; and it was pinned up so her swan neck was showing. She looked so young and desirable that everything about her he'd felt when he first saw her he now felt. If Sandy had been there then to ask why he had slept with her that time he wouldn't have needed to have said anything at all, he would simply have pointed to her and Sandy would have understood.

'Sorry I'm late.' Miranda's kiss just missed his cheek. Gordon had the urge to pull her towards him and kiss her full on the lips. As usual, by the time he'd considered the potential outcome, the impulse had passed. It struck Gordon as he fetched a gin and tonic from the bar that perhaps in a parallel world a more contented version of himself existed: one which had acted on all of those still-born impulses.

Gordon was gratified to see that Miranda still drank the same way. She sipped and, between each sip, blinked – a nervous habit she'd never been able to cure herself of. Then, with a 'Don't tell Stephen,' she pulled out her cigarettes, lit one, and drew needily on it.

'When did you start?' It was the wrong question. Miranda didn't answer but looked quickly away to hide her annoyance. She hadn't come to fight.

'I'm sorry,' Gordon said.

'Look. Let's make a pact shall we? Let's just accept that what's done is done. I'll never be able to understand it, but I'm sure you had your reasons.'

'Well . . .' But Gordon wasn't, at this point, being called on to give his carefully prepared disclaimer.

'No.' Miranda held up her hand to cut him off. 'What I'm saying is that I don't want you to spend all night apologising. I don't want to hear it. We won't be able to move on and do what we have to do if you're being sorry all the time. Especially when you don't really mean it.'

'Okay.' Gordon breathed easier.

'Are we going to eat, or are we going to sit here all night?' Gordon heard echoes of an old irritability.

'No. I thought we could go to the Italian. You know, by the bank. I haven't booked or anything.'

'It's closed down.' Miranda said with some relish, or so Gordon thought.

'Oh.'

'Yes, they went out of business in the summer.'

'Shame.'

'Yes.'

'Well is there anywhere else we used to go?'

There was nowhere else. Or, if there was, they both agreed that it was probably a better idea for them to find somewhere they hadn't been before. They walked arm-in-arm along the street of bright restaurants, busy with belonging people, and were both painfully reminded that it was very much a ritual from their past. Occasionally they'd get a baby-sitter on the spur of the moment, dress up and go out without booking. Then they'd walk for an hour until they could find a place they both liked the look of. But somehow they were always searching for something different. Miranda wanted life, fun, a busy Greek taverna. Gordon wanted the more intimate pleasures of a smaller, darker, more discreet restaurant. Miranda had always wanted to join in, Gordon, to be left out. They often compromised by finding somewhere that would suit Miranda, but then sat on the sidelines and spectated, which satisfied neither of them: Gordon would feel guilty, Miranda frustrated.

'Perhaps we stopped trying,' Miranda said as they started on the second bottle of house red. They were in a badly lit corner of a new Greek restaurant. Miranda was eating a dubious lump of lamb called Kleftika. Gordon was eating a dry and tasteless kebab. The young Cypriot waitress with eyes the colour of olives and a starched cotton shirt was fiercely attentive. She seemed to appear between each mouthful to check that everything was alright, as though she'd been charged with monitoring the progress of her father's food through each key stage of the digestive process.

'I suppose we did,' Gordon said, whimsically. He was now too drunk to make any credible emotional responses.

'I wonder if it's too late,' Miranda said, almost to herself, and, when Gordon didn't reply, 'What do you think of Stephen?'

'Well . . .' He waited, reasoning that there must be something good he could think of. 'I think he's. I mean I'm sure he's . . .'

'He makes me feel good about myself.' That was all Miranda wanted to say; she wasn't really interested in Gordon's opinion.

'Good. I mean, if that's what you need, then good.'

'Don't be so shitty. You know what I mean.'

'I mean, what you're saying here is that I didn't. Is that it?' Gordon pushed his plate away. The kebab languished like a turd on the plate.

'If you want the truth, then yes I am.'

'I wasn't aware that my role in life was to bolster your fragile self-esteem.'

'You really have become bitter, haven't you?'

'I'm sorry. I didn't mean that.'

'It's alright, Gordon. You can't hurt me any more. I've become immune.'

'It takes two to tango, Miranda,' Gordon said solemnly.

Miranda laughed and choked on her lamb. 'What the hell is that supposed to mean?'

'Well . . .' but Gordon couldn't remember the point he was trying to make.

'No. Go on.'

'Oh . . .' Gordon waved imprecisely into the air. 'Christ knows. I suppose what I meant to say was that it was both of us. I mean, neither of us was any good at, you know, what you were saying about . . .'

'Bolstering each other's fragile self-esteem.'

'Exactly.' Gordon pounced on the point like a bar-room barrister. 'Exactly.'

'I never thought you were fragile. Never.'

'Yes, well . . . I was.' And the realisation surprised him.

'Really?'

'Really.'

'I never thought that. I didn't know you very well, did I?'

'You did. I think we both did, I mean, at one time, know each other. At the beginning. But I think we changed. I think we lost touch with each other.'

'Yes. We did.'

'You see I don't think anybody can hope to know

anybody else. Not in any . . . significant way. All you can hope for is to know a bit. But it's the bit that the other person allows. Do you understand?'

'Yes, don't worry, you've not lost me yet.'

'But, where was I? Yes, but, you see, what happens is that as you change you have less control over the bit you show. Then, puff! It's all gone in a puff of smoke.'

Gordon was about to develop the point further when the waitress bustled up at a speed that led him to imagine she had been watching them through a telescope. 'Is everything alright?' The clap of his hands that had accompanied his puff of smoke had brought her over.

'No,' Gordon said, looking at the table with theatrical horror. 'I think someone's crapped on my plate.'

'Jesus,' Miranda said, and put down her knife and fork. The waitress looked at the plate, at Gordon, then spat something at him in Greek before storming through the swing doors to the kitchen. Voices were immediately raised, each one competing both in tone and volume for dominance.

'Well it looks like it, you have to admit,' Gordon said.

Miranda rummaged for her cigarettes. At the next table a corpulent woman with a ginger moustache and doughy arms tutted as she lit up. The attentive, emaciated terrier of a man with her immediately took up the cry and called for the waitress. Miranda blew the smoke coolly across their stuffed vine leaves. 'You're so . . . fucking determined to spoil everything, aren't you.'

'Not on purpose,' Gordon said weakly.

'It is. You always do it on purpose. You just don't realise that you are.'

'It was a joke!'

'Not funny, Gordon. You're not funny.' Miranda slid with a half bow from behind the table and walked out, stopping briefly to glare at the woman at the next table. Gordon left thirty pounds on his plate and chased after her, but when he got out onto the street she was gone. He walked slowly back the way they had come and found Miranda leaning in the recess of a shop doorway and crying. Gordon tried to put his arms round her but she pushed him away.

'I'm sorry.' He stood facing her; four feet away, just out of reach. He felt the emotional impotence of an adolescent.

'Why did you do it, Gordon?'

'I told you. It was supposed to be a joke.'

'Not that! Why did you leave us? Why!' Her tears had been an overture to hysteria.

'I don't know.'

'Why! It wasn't so bad, was it? We could have worked things out. Yes I was angry with you. Yes I was hurt. But you just walked away. You left me before I had any chance to be angry with you. We used to talk. We always used to talk about everything. You took everything. Everything. And you weren't even there to talk it out with.' Miranda went for him, slapping fiercely at his face. The stone on her wedding ring cut the skin above his eye. 'Why?'

'I'm sorry.'

'I don't want you to be sorry! I want to know why.'

'I don't know why.'

'You do. You fucking do.'

'I'm sorry.'

'Why do you hate everybody? Where's the . . . joy in you?'

'I wish I knew.' Gordon cowered beneath the protection of his arms as the verbal and physical torrent continued to assault him. The blows rained for a while in silent but increasing intensity.

'Why do you consider yourself better than the entire human race? Why?'

'I don't.'

Miranda paused, then, when his guard was down, slapped him again. 'Don't lie!' This time she hit him in the chest with her fist.

'It's not something I want to feel . . . I can't help what I feel.'

'Yes you can. You have no compassion!'

'I have!' Gordon caught Miranda's fist in his palm just before it connected a more considered blow on his nose. She pulled it away and hammered it into the wall.

'You have not. Believe me. You do not have compassion.'

'Well what do you want me to say, Miranda? Eh?' Gordon stepped back out of range again. 'Do you think I feel what I feel just to spite you? Is that it?'

'No. I think you're beyond help. I really do,' Miranda snarled and licked the blood from her forearm. Gordon couldn't help but be impressed by her rage. They hadn't fought like this for as long as he could remember. But she was calmer now.

A cab driver who had pulled up to watch drove away. Three shirt-sleeved louts moved on after calling encouragement to Miranda. Gordon felt the blood coagulating like glue on his forehead. Miranda handed him a paper handkerchief and he wiped it away.

'I'm sorry,' Gordon began carefully. 'I know we agreed not to talk about it. But I really am sorry.'

'Please. I don't want to hear it.' Miranda was pale, wrung dry with her anger.

'Listen. I want to say something. I want to say . . .' Miranda waited, but it was just out of reach, something too dark to contemplate. What Gordon thought, what he felt; an ache that had become a pain that wouldn't go away: an old wound that wouldn't heal.

Miranda took Gordon's hand. 'There's something I have to tell you.'

'Yes?' he said, bringing up her hand to rest it on his cheek.

'Stephen's asked me to marry him.'

They walked back to the pub and started again. Both were aware of what the other was feeling, almost more acutely than what they, themselves, felt. Whatever had gone wrong between them, they had never lost that connection.

'Do you love him?' Gordon said, when they were back at their table. The question triggered the pain in his chest he felt whenever he thought of his wife and Stephen in bed together: noisy, ecstatic, teasing, trying all the things they should have tried together but were too ashamed to admit they wanted.

'Yes. I think, I think I do.' Miranda seemed to be contemplating the possibility for the first time. 'He says he loves me, but I don't think he really knows.'

'But why marry him? I thought people didn't get married any more. That's what the papers say anyway.'

'Because it feels right. I can't explain it, Gordon, and this is not meant to hurt you. But I feel as though I've been given another chance. He makes me feel wanted – alive, he values me. It's not something I have to demand from him. It's just something he does. It's not just the sex.'

'I see,' Gordon said, wanting and, equally, not wanting to know about the sex.

'I don't blame you. I'm sure I failed you too. That's what I mean about trying, but I'm nearly forty. I think I have to take this chance . . .' She waited for a response. 'Tell me what you're thinking.'

'I don't know.' Gordon continued to stare gloomily into his beer. 'Too many things. Nothing at all. I don't know.'

'Come on. Tell me.'

'Sometimes . . . sometimes I feel a part of me is split off. Like a satellite or a balloon or something, and it just hovers above me and watches. And nothing can touch it, or hurt it. And sometimes I feel like I've climbed up the rope and all of me is in it. That's how I feel now. Stupid, isn't it?'

'What?'

'Thoughts like that. Sad thoughts. Thoughts of a sad man, a pathetic . . .'

'Stop it. Stop doing it to yourself. Just tell me what you see when you look down from that balloon. Do you mind about what I've told you?' She spoke with a timidity that Gordon misread as tenderness.

'Yes. I do. And I think you're making a mistake. But that's up to you.'

'You don't like him.'

'No. No, I don't. I think he's . . . bitter. I think he wants you because . . . no, it's not up to me to make those judgements.'

'No. It's not. I'm not going to defend him to you because I don't have to, but I will say that when he's alone he's very different.'

'I'll take your word for it.'

'Come and sit here.' Miranda patted the seat beside her. A cloud of dust rose from the mauve draylon. Gordon sat close to her and she took his hand. 'We'll never lose touch. I promise you that. And I know it's going to be difficult but we're just going to have to work at it.'

'I'm prepared to do that. I just hope he doesn't make it too difficult for you . . . I want to make love to you.' Gordon clenched Miranda's hand tightly. He had never felt desire as sharply. Only now he was losing Miranda did he know how much he wanted her to stay. Habit had fallen over their marriage like dust over a closed room of furniture. Now the habit was gone and the dust blown away, Gordon could see his face reflected in the shine again. But it was too late.

'I can't, Gordon.' Miranda sighed hard.

'Because of him?'

'No. Not just because of him. You don't listen, do you. I said I was in love with him. I think I am. I can't divorce sex from love. That's something you've never entirely understood. I just can't do it.'

'So you don't love me,' Gordon stated slowly.

'Yes. I love you. I'll always love you. I'm just not in love with you.'

'Forgive me if I don't get the difference.'

'I think we should go before we get into something we might regret.'

Gordon drained his glass and followed Miranda out of the pub.

THREE

ON CHRISTMAS EVE Gordon called Miranda and told her he'd decided not to go down to Hampshire with the family but would spend the following day with Monnery and Jan. Then he called back and spoke to Pen to explain why. Pen said that she understood and seemed more concerned for him than herself. When he woke at three a.m. on Christmas morning Gordon knew he had no intention of going anywhere. He switched on his small portable television and watched the end of an old American film. The continuity announcer wished the nation a Happy Christmas and Gordon wished him one back. Then he made himself a cup of coffee and sat by the window waiting for the dawn. It came slowly, edging up like a rising tide behind the terraced streets, light slowly saturating the shadows away. The pavements were white with powdered frost, unblemished by footprints.

At a little before nine Gordon found an envelope of photographs in his suitcase and laid the pictures of his children on the bed. Then he went back to bed and slept fitfully through the dreadful day.

At ten o'clock the next morning there was a knock on his door. He opened it to Clive in a peaked cap jangling his loose change in his pocket and dangling a large bunch of car keys.

'I've come to fetch you,' Clive said breezily. 'Orders from the boss.'

'What?'

'Come on you lazy sod. Get dressed. I'm taking you to Piran's.'

They arrived at the house at midday. Gordon had been there only once before when Piran's parents had organised his wedding reception in a marquee behind the house. It had rained all day and by the evening the humidity in the tent was so severe that a number of the younger guests had stripped to their underwear to dance. Someone cut their foot on a champagne glass, and a trestle table was pulled over, spilling cold meat onto the wooden floor. Gordon's hazy memories of Piran and Sandy's wedding were of a group of semi-naked people jiving and slipping on a dance floor made treacherous by ham and chicken fat. But the red-brick house with its teetering chimneys and its broad-fronted air of benevolence had been built for days like that; the building sang like a well-tuned piano to the sound of voices raised in joy.

The first person Gordon saw when he walked in was Mr Blake. He was standing with his brown overcoat on in the large hall waiting to go out. He looked like a suit of armour: immobile but potentially lethal. Party chatter spilt from the drawing room at the back of the house. Anne came out with a glass in her hand and greeted Gordon with a kiss, a stale cocktail of alcohol and cigarette smoke. She handed the glass of Pimms to him and before he could greet Blake led him by the arm to an upstairs room. Gordon sat on the bed while she opened his case.

'You haven't brought much,' Anne said, hanging his single white shirt in the wardrobe.

'Well I'm not going to stay for long. Clive said I should come so I thought I'd show willing.' Gordon fought to keep the dullness from his voice. Now he was here, he was intent on not being miserable. Miranda's accusation the previous week had gnawed away at his self-confidence ever since.

'It's not the same without you, you know.' Anne sat beside him on the bed. He was immediately engulfed in the thick fog of her perfume. It reminded Gordon of what his mother used to smell like when she came in to kiss him goodnight. 'We've all behaved terribly badly, haven't we?'

'I wouldn't say so.'

'Hardly what you would call friends, are we? I mean, Mr Blake's here so there seemed no reason not to invite you too. Come on. Come down and meet everybody. We're all trying to get into the spirit of things. Piran's insisting we all dress for lunch.'

'That's handy.' Gordon looked at his shirt dangling alone in the wardrobe.

Anne went over and opened another thick sunburst walnut door. Hanging inside was a plastic-covered black tail suit. 'He's thought of everything.'

'Alright. I'll be down in a minute. I'll just finish this, then I'll get dressed.' Gordon raised his glass.

'Dutch courage?'

'Yes.'

Anne closed the door behind her. The room was intensely hot; an ancient radiator hissed a needle of steam from a valve. Gordon went over to the window and looked out at the lawn. The quiet woman was standing alone on the wide grey steps which led down to the lower level of the garden; the formal flower beds were glazed with frost, and mist cloaked the far end from sight. The woman was wearing a long black velvet dress but she had a red scarf tied at her throat. It matched the colour of her lipstick, which stood out bright against the marble whiteness of her face and the pallor of the winter morning. She was smoking a cigarette in a long holder. Gordon tried to open the window to call to her. But when he'd released the rusty catch and got it open he realised he didn't know what he wanted to shout so he leaned on the window ledge and just watched her for a while.

Gordon stamped out of his shapeless jeans and slipped into the formal constraints of the dark suit. As he put it on he felt better. It forced him to stand straighter and almost demanded that he strike a pose in it. Looking in the mirror he encountered a far more preferable version of himself. He looked almost presentable.

Blake was still waiting beside the front doors when Gordon came down.

'How are you?' Gordon said, careful to approach him from the front and not creep up on him.

'I'm going out,' Blake said. 'To the shops.'

'You don't have to. They have food here.'

Gordon could see Blake slowly processing the information, then he demanded, 'Can you tell me how to get to the shops?'

'Just go down the drive. Turn left. There's a village about a mile away.'

'Thank you.' Blake seemed to be waiting for Gordon to dismiss him.

'I'll come with you.'

'No.'

'Well make sure you come back.'

Blake executed a stiff bow and walked out. Gordon straightened his bow tie, fixed a convivial smile on his face and walked into the drawing room.

The small group was dwarfed by the room even though the parallel gilt-framed mirrors were doing their best to make up the numbers. Miranda was sitting on a chaise longue with

Ben who was sucking his fingers and looking tired. Pen was kneeling at the stool of the concert grand and flicking through some sheet music. Stephen was beside the tall doors looking moodily out. Piran and Sandy, and Clive and Anne were sitting round a green baize card table. Piran flexed a pack of new cards then shuffled them and dealt. The quiet man hovered behind Stephen as though he was trying to follow his line of sight. The quiet woman was still smoking and striking an enigmatic pose on the steps.

Piran was the first to see Gordon. He laid his cards down then advanced on him with his hand outstretched. Apart from the night in the park it was the first time the two had met since Piran had given him the black eye. When they met half-way across the room the expansiveness of Piran's gesture seemed to have been re-thought. As he took Gordon's right hand in his, his left folded over it. The 'Good to see you, Gordon' was pitched too low for it to have merely symbolic meaning. After that, Gordon was hugged, embraced, kissed and slapped on the back by the rest of them in a scrum of self-congratulatory greetings. He had been missed, he could tell, because as soon as the backslapping was finished everybody seemed to relax, helped themselves to another drink and looked less determined to enjoy themselves against the odds.

The quiet woman walked in when he had been assimilated into the group. She caught his eye and they exchanged a look which seemed to suggest a shared understanding of what was going on in the room. She looked ill. She had lost weight round her face where she did not have weight to lose. When she caught Gordon staring at her later, she looked away quickly as if he had seen something the others had not. But Piran was the major revelation. His hair had turned completely grey but his face was even greyer. He had aged ten years, something Gordon had missed in the half light of the park that evening with Blake.

'We're seeing the old place off,' Piran said for Gordon's benefit but also to remind the rest of them why they were dressed up. 'In memory of Pops and the splendid Christmases I remember as a child.' He smiled, his eyes misty with drunken melancholy.

'Hear hear,' Clive chipped in, 'I'll drink to that.'

Gordon did his best to catch up with the rest of them but the air of despair was soon back among them. Gordon's arrival had been merely a diversion. Like a mass hysteria there was an almost palpable air of imminent disaster. Gordon wanted to take Miranda and the children and run before the time-bomb exploded and the building was reduced to rubble. His concern reached Miranda who took him from Anne's side and walked him to the other end of the room. Separated couples were at least allowed the space to be alone together.

'I don't know what's going on,' Miranda whispered, then laughed as if Gordon had told a joke.

'Why did you do that?' Gordon looked into the mirror, convinced for a moment that somebody had come up behind them and goosed her.

'I don't know. It's this place. Everybody's at screaming point. It's dreadful. Piran and Sandy had the most almighty row last night. It woke everybody up. She was screaming at him. I think he must have hit her or something. Anyway, Stephen went out to see what was going on and Piran told him he was going to kill himself.'

'God.'

'Anne thinks he's going mad like Pops. He looks awful, doesn't he?'

'Well I don't see there's anything we can do about it.'

165

'No. I don't suppose we can leave. I think we should stay
— if only for Sandy's sake.'

'Yes, I mean the baby could be along any minute couldn't
it.'

'Not if you go on the official dates, no.' Miranda gave
Gordon one of her looks before going over to join Stephen
beside the window. He said something sharp to her. Gordon
saw her wince at the ferocity of it. Then she took his arm to
calm him. Ben had gone to sleep on the sofa. The quiet
woman and her husband were at the long table helping
themselves to another gin; the quiet woman's hand shook as
she poured. Anne and Clive were trying to make conversation about the family portraits in the room but nobody was
in the mood to chip in. Piran joined Gordon by the
fireplace, a bottle of brandy in his hand. He diluted Gordon's
Pimms with a generous measure of it.

'Thank Christ you're here,' Piran whispered.

'Good of you to invite me, I mean, under the circumstances.'

'Bollocks to that, old man. Water under the bridge. No,
it's about Sandy.'

'What?'

'I think she's going off her trolley.'

Sandy was stroking Pen's hair as they talked at the card
table.

'Is she?' Gordon said. She looked calm enough to him,
even more serene than the week before when he'd met her
in the pub.

'She wakes up screaming. Every night. Then she accuses
me of touching her up in her sleep. I tell you, the sooner this
sprog arrives the happier I'll be.'

'Well how are you bearing up?'

'Musn't grumble.'

'No. Tell me.'

166

Piran tapped his chest. 'Nothing worse than a touch of indigestion. That's all. I'll live. Come on, let's have a sing-song before lunch.'

'I'm glad you came,' Pen said. Gordon had followed Pen when she left the room. They were chatting in the comparative privacy of the bathroom. Pen dried her face on a lush white towel then anchored her arms round Gordon's waist. Gordon kissed her on the top of her head, realising as he did so that he hardly had to bend at all now to reach her.

'How are you?'

'I'm alright.'

Gordon tilted Pen's chin up. 'Tell me.'

'I'm alright unless somebody asks me if I'm alright.'

'And then?'

'Then I feel sad. It's alright to feel sad. Mummy said so . . . she said it was better to feel sad than nothing.'

'And do you think she feels sad?'

'Yes. All the time. All the time . . . Have you had a look round the house?'

'No. I've only just got here.'

'Come on. I want to show you something.' Pen took Gordon's hand and they walked down an uncarpeted corridor which ran off the hallway and towards the heart of the house. There was little light and the central heating didn't extend this far. The corridor was lit by a series of bare bulbs strung between flex and attached to the walls beside the fixtures of the old gas lamps. At the end Pen led them down some steps into a small, bitterly cold chapel which reminded Gordon of an old court house. The family pews were raised above the level of the bare wooden benches. The room was illuminated by the daylight coming through the stained-glass windows. The windows were dark and ornate; scarlet and blue with jewels of yellow. Pen walked to the far wall and held her palm against it.

'Feel it.'

Gordon's leather soles echoed loudly on the stone floor as he went to join her. He felt the wall. It was warm and there was a faint pulse. Gordon pulled his hand sharply away.

'Why is it hot?' Pen said.

'God knows. There must be a heating pipe buried in the wall, I suppose.' Gordon looked up at the ceiling but could see no evidence of any piping. He looked at the windows above him. He had taken the stained-glass figures to be representations of the saints. On closer inspection, he saw that some were not. The yellow cross at the centre of one window turned out to be a woman staked out naked and splayed; a beast was at her feet with cloven hooves and the torso of a man. Gordon felt the wall again. The pulsing seemed to have intensified. Pen was resting her cheek against it. Gordon took her hand and led her back to the dining room making her promise not to go into the chapel again.

After a lunch of game pie Piran announced that he would be leading a walk round the village, through the woods, and back to the house over the hill. There would be a stop at the pub and Wellington boots were recommended. The walk, however, was not compulsory. He then went to get changed but it was only when Sandy followed him out a few minutes later that the atmosphere lightened in the drawing room. Anne voiced what they were all feeling: 'Well we can't all not go, can we? I mean I could do with an hour or so's sleep after last night.'

'I don't mind going,' the quiet woman said.

'I'll go,' Gordon chipped in, only because of the prospect of the pub. 'How about you, Pen?'

'No way.' The city child didn't look up from her book.

A number of the others were already asleep in the armchairs.

'Miranda?'

Miranda looked at Stephen who was glaring darkly into the middle distance. 'No, I think we'll stay.'

'Fine.' Gordon went in search of Mr Blake and found him sitting at the table in the large kitchen. He was eating his pie from the cellophane packet and still had his coat on. The cook was at the range inserting wads of stuffing into the various orifices of a series of white-fleshed birds lying next to each other in a large pan. Gordon invited Blake to join the walk but he declined without explanation or excuse.

Piran led off from the house in a waxed jacket and a pair of sturdy Wellington boots. He strode slightly ahead of Sandy who kept pace with him but didn't put on the extra speed necessary to catch him up. Gordon and the quiet woman lagged behind, just out of earshot. They walked down the drive, through the gates, and turned left along the quiet, narrow lane towards the village. The skies were unblemished by vapour trails and there was not even the distant sound of cars. A strand of unmatched birds loitered loutishly on the telephone cables; at Piran's approach they lifted off and rose away like specks of soot caught in the wind. A little further along they passed a wire-fenced garden. A peacock appeared from behind a sculpted bush, turned and fanned its tail like a magician flourishing a pack of cards. Piran and Sandy walked on; Gordon and the quiet woman stopped to watch. Until that point they had not said much but the spontaneous display of beauty gave Gordon the spur to ask her how she was.

'I don't want to talk about me.'

'Why not?'

'I talk to the doctors all the time about me. I want to talk about you.'

'Alright.'

They moved off and Gordon took the woman's arm.

'Tell me how you're intending to get Miranda back.'

'I'm not. She's marrying Stephen. That's that.'

'Is it?'

'Of course it is. She's a grown woman. She's seen something she wants and nothing I say is going to change her mind. I mean, I really don't see what I can do about it.'

'For a relatively connected man, Gordon, you really are dim sometimes.'

'Am I?' Gordon had forgotten quite how much he enjoyed talking to the quiet woman whose name he had, as usual, forgotten.

'Of course you are. She wants you to go after her.'

'I don't think so.'

'Look. This is not about your pride now. You have to put that aside and tell her how much you want her. It's quite simple. She'd much rather be with you than Stephen.'

'I don't think so.'

'Look, I know the sex may be good.' Gordon flinched. 'But that won't last for ever. He's very selfish, and very immature.'

'Yes, I thought that but I didn't really think I could say it, I mean . . .'

'Of course you can't say it, you stupid man. You can't desert her then come back and tell her the man she's chosen to replace you was the wrong choice.'

'Well then . . . so what else can I do?'

'Bide your time. Be yourself. She just has to be made to feel you want her. That you love her. That you still, I don't know, desire her for Christ's sake. You do, don't you?'

'Of course I do.'

'Well it all seems pretty straightforward to me but then I'm not a man, am I . . . All I would say is that a woman has to feel wanted; valued; respected. I know you probably feel you need all of those things too but your needs are going to have to wait. If you make her feel those things she'll do the same to you.'

'Mm.' Gordon considered it for a while, then said, 'It seems a bit like a game to me. I mean we're supposed to be mature adults.'

'Nobody's mature when it comes to needs. And it isn't a game, not in the sense you mean. If anything it's an equation, a science . . . I don't know . . .' The woman's breathing had become laboured. She stopped to regain her breath, leaning some of her weight on Gordon's chest, her other hand on the cold stone wall of the churchyard.

'You're really quite ill, aren't you?' Gordon said.

'Let's just say that in the time I have left I intend to make people like you see how valuable life really is. It's quite easy to forget when you take it for granted. Christ, I'm beginning to sound like one of those Californian self-help books. I must be in a bad way.'

They walked on but Piran and Sandy were now out of sight. When they reached the pub they went in and sat on tall stools at the bar.

The quiet woman ruminated over her gin. '. . . The thing is that you can't quite believe it's ever going to happen to you. I mean, life feels like such a right when you have it that . . . that you only realise it was a privilege when it becomes threatened.'

'I am so sorry,' Gordon said and took the woman in his arms. She laid her cheek on his shoulder but would not cry. The landlord found something to do at the far end of the bar.

'Sometimes you can live more in a brief moment than in an entire life. Piran and Sandy are beyond help. Anne and

Clive I don't care enough about, but I do care about you and Miranda, and I want to see you two back together. Tell her that you love her. Tell her even if it hurts you to tell her. It will get easier. Joy is as easy to find as pain, it just takes a little more work to hold on to. Life is a privilege, Gordon. Use it and stop feeling so bloody sorry for yourself.'

'Alright. I hear you ... so tell me about your brief moment.'

'Oh no. Oh no, that's private. I take that with me, my desert island moment.'

FOUR

GORDON WOKE WITH a jolt when he heard the first scream. He grabbed for his watch. It was a little before three. He had been drinking all the previous day and the dehydration hit him as he stood up to pull on his jeans. In the corridor outside the room he collided with Clive who was tangled in a dressing gown. The arm was inside out and he was fighting with it as though he was trying to escape from a straitjacket.

'I don't know about you,' Clive said, 'but I'm not letting him get away with it again. Are you coming?'

They jogged down the corridor. As they passed Pen's room, she appeared and Gordon stopped to usher her back in. When her head touched the pillow again, her eyes closed and she was immediately asleep. Gordon caught up with Clive standing outside Piran's room with his ear pressed to the door.

'It's gone quiet,' Clive said, looking to Gordon for the next decision. Blake appeared from the far end of the corridor and sailed past them like a ghost.

Then they heard another scream, a deep-throated resonant scream of pain, guttural and animalistic. The bed creaked.

'Well?' Clive said, hopelessly.

173

'Knock,' Gordon instructed, and Clive tapped on the door, prompting another creak of the bed then silence.

'Who is it?' Piran's disturbed voice issued from inside, and at the same moment Miranda appeared. Despite all that was going on around him Gordon knew that she was naked inside the short dressing gown. He felt a stab of desire. Miranda caught his look and made sure that Gordon saw she had acknowledged it. Stephen then appeared, tugging on his pyjama trousers. His penis protruded from the fly, half-erect.

'Well?' Clive said again, now renouncing all responsibility.

'Ask them if everything's all right,' Miranda whispered, huddling closer to Gordon and closer to the door. Stephen took hold of her arm.

Gordon cleared his throat of the salt saliva of stale whisky and called out, 'It's Gordon. Are you alright?'

They heard a swift exchange from behind the door, then Piran in a more controlled voice assured them that all was well. Gordon shrugged and looked at Miranda who had by now freed herself from Stephen's hold. She said, 'We can't just go, can we? I mean what if Sandy's hurt or something?'

Gordon shrugged again, then the door opened a crack and Piran's white face took in the corridor group.

'What's going on in there?' Gordon said pompously.

'It's Sandy. Just another nightmare. Everything's under control. Go back to bed.' Piran tried to pull the door closed but Miranda blocked it with her foot.

'Look.' Miranda pushed the door open a little further, Sandy was lying with her back to them. Her shoulders were shaking. 'Let me in please.' Piran backed off and Miranda went round to Sandy's side of the bed, knelt down and pushed the hair from her eyes.

'I can't do this any more,' Sandy whispered. 'I just can't.' Gordon looked round the semi-darkness of the room. There was a camp bed beneath the window, the sheets pulled down. Sandy's clothes were strewn over the floor. White pills and rolls of ten pound notes were scattered on the dressing table.

'What can't you do?' Miranda prompted.

'Live. Just live. That's all. I feel so . . . so finished.' Miranda stroked her head.

Piran's eyes filled with tears. He sat on the bed then rolled onto his side, hunched his knees to his chest and began to cry. Gordon knelt beside him.

Then Sandy screamed again and the proximity to it prompted Miranda to scream as loud.

'I think it's the baby,' Miranda said as liquid darkened the back of Sandy's nightdress. Piran tried to stand. The colour had drained from his face.

'Christ,' Clive said.

'Call an ambulance.' Stephen pushed Clive towards the door; he ran from the room. Miranda wiped Sandy's brow, Sandy was holding her wrist. Gordon was kneeling over Piran trying to loosen his collar. Piran said something. It sounded like 'Don't leave me.' Then he closed his eyes and slept.

It was light when Gordon arrived back from the hospital. He found Stephen in the hall, sitting on an up-ended suitcase and looking gloomily into space.

'Well?' Stephen said.

'A boy. Seven pounds. Mother and son doing well. Father admitted with exhaustion. They've given him something to knock him out for a few days.' The setting seemed to dictate that he call the rest of the guests into the drawing room and announce not a birth but a death, and also a motive and a suspect.

'He'll pull through,' Stephen said dispassionately.

'Yes. He will. They both will . . .' The house felt lighter than the day before. 'Are you off then?'

'Yes.'

'I see.'

'Well it's pretty clear you don't want me around, do you?'

'No. Of course I don't. But then I wouldn't, would I?'

'Not just you. It's solidarity of the inner circle and all that.' He seemed younger and less sure of himself; somehow he seemed to want Gordon to challenge his assertion.

'Oh, you're feeling left out of the game, are you? Is that why you've been looking so miserable since I got here?'

'None of your business.'

'Is Miranda leaving too?' Gordon said, hardly daring to hope.

'No.'

'Oh . . . right.' Of the reasons that sprang into Gordon's mind, Stephen immediately voiced the most gratifying one.

'It's over. We're finished . . .' Stephen watched for a response but Gordon was too numb and too tired for the elation to show. 'You can have her back,' Stephen said bitterly. 'I've got all I want from her.'

'It wasn't that way,' Miranda said, coming out of the drawing room. Stephen blushed.

'I see,' Gordon said.

'I told him I couldn't live with him any longer.'

'Well . . . good.' Gordon's look switched between the two of them. Miranda was replaying the conversation for his benefit but also to shame Stephen into an apology.

'Because I was going back to my husband. I wanted to live with a man. Not a boy. That's what I told him. Isn't it, Stephen?'

'I don't remember any complaints on that score before, Miranda. You know you'll regret it.' But the final lunge lacked conviction and Miranda looked at him with pity. The day had taken a toll on Stephen too; he looked tired and utterly lost.

'I certainly don't regret it now.' Miranda went to Gordon and stood shoulder-to-shoulder with him.

'Habit is no substitute for passion,' Stephen said.

'I think I'm capable of passion.' Gordon threaded his arm round Miranda's waist. Her flinch was involuntary, she didn't really want to be touched by anyone at that moment, but Stephen saw it.

'You're dead from the neck down, Gordon,' Stephen said. 'I'll always be in your bed. Just remember that.'

'Go now, please,' Miranda said.

Stephen picked up his case and walked out. Gordon was left with his arm round Miranda trying to shake off the awful image of Stephen and his wife making love. It cut into his heart and deeper into his pride. He knew it would diminish, but he also knew it would never entirely leave him.

'I'm never going to talk about him,' Miranda said, pulling gently away. 'I'm not going to deny what he meant to me. And I won't let you blame me for it.'

'Of course not.'

'We just need to start again. And try harder.'

'Yes,' Gordon said. 'We must. Try harder, I mean.'

Blake emerged from the chapel corridor. 'The wall is no longer pulsing,' he announced. 'The pulsing stopped at three forty-five a.m.' He cleared his throat. 'I have looked into the room above the chapel but can find no evidence of heating pipes. I have also examined the exterior of the wall. There is nothing there that would cause a regular pulsing. From this I can only conclude some supernatural activity.' He bowed. 'I thank you for your attention.' It was the longest speech Gordon had ever heard him make.

'Thank you, Blake,' Gordon said. 'I'll let Piran know when I go in to see him.'

Blake walked off and up the stairs.

Pen, who had been watching them from the gallery, knew it was now time to leave her parents in peace. Her father was finally back from Egypt, the awful Stephen was gone, and now all she had to do was to get rid of that embarrassing painting of her mother from the living room and everything would be back to normal.

FIVE

SANDY WAS BALANCING the baby on her knee and looking rapidly between its face and Gordon's. He was sitting on the sofa opposite. They were back in London and Gordon had called in on his way from school. It was the third time in as many days that, drawn by a sense of paternity and inquisitiveness, he had delayed his journey home.

'He doesn't look like me at all,' Gordon said. He had always found babies to be ugly, except his own. This child seemed too large to be his. It looked like Mr Magoo.

'He's got your eyes,' Sandy said. 'Other than that, he could easily be . . .'

'Yes. Can I hold him?'

'Not while he's quiet if you don't mind.'

'Of course not.' Gordon began drumming the taut fabric on the arm of the sofa with his fingers. 'Is there anything I can do?'

'No. Not here. I think you'd be better off sorting things out at home, wouldn't you?'

'We're taking things gently. Step-by-step.'

'Does Miranda know you're here?'

'Yes. She thought it would be a good idea.'

'Have you told her you're the father?'

'Of course not. I think she'd rather not know. I mean, I think she knows. I'm sure she knows. But unless either you or I tell her she can pretend she doesn't.'

'That's your way of sorting things out, is it?'

'Well . . . yes.' Gordon had found that 'sorting things out' was similar to 'going through things' but much more intense. Miranda was keen to 'wipe the slate clean', to 'start again'. She was full of hope that the patterns they had fallen into could be broken if they both made the effort. But making an effort was exhausting. They were currently being unbearably polite with each other and having long circular conversations about their own faults and failings. They'd booked a weekend in Venice together to have another go at having another go.

The baby began gurgling. Sandy hoisted it onto her shoulder like a hod of bricks, stood up and began a routine of semi genuflections. The gurgling stopped.

'I wanted to ask you about that night.' Gordon stood too out of a sense of politeness.

'I don't want to talk about it.'

'Fine.'

'Everything came to a head. That's all. Piran never really sorted out what he felt about Pops dying like that. He feels responsible for his mother. And his brother. And there was simply nothing left for me. Let alone him. He's in the right place. He'll be fine.'

'Does he want visitors?'

'No. Only me and his little boy. It's giving him something to live for. I like him more for it. I think we'll get through, though. Here. Take him.' Sandy handed the child to Gordon as though she'd suddenly lost interest in him. She sat, careful of her stitches, breathed through the pain, then relaxed. 'Look, do you mind if I say something?'

'Of course not.' Gordon was pacing a tiny circle on the

Persian carpet. For part of the rotation he could see his reflection in the mirror above the fire. He didn't look right holding the baby but couldn't quite work out why. Then he knew: it was because he looked like the child's grandfather. His expression was fond enough, but there was impatience in it, and a look of relief which sprang from the fact that he was providing only temporary care.

'I don't want you to come round here for a while.'

'Oh.' Gordon stopped turning. 'Why not?'

'Because . . . because each time you come, I think you're going to stay. I mean, I know you're not really, but I have this sort of daydream that you will. I dream of all kinds of things . . . that you are bathing him. And that you put him to bed . . . you know.'

'Christ. I had no idea. I'm sorry. I'm really sorry.'

The child was asleep. Gordon laid him in the cot and kissed his forehead.

'I'm feeling very vulnerable at the moment. When you're here it sort of lifts. But when you leave it's worse. Much worse than before you came. Will you hold me please?' Sandy was reaching towards him. Gordon knelt down and took her in his arms.

'I've been selfish, haven't I?'

'But I don't really want you here, you see . . . In this dream it's twenty years ago. And it's summer. And our lives are going to be wonderful and full of . . . meaning, and joy; real joy. Because we're strong. Not just together. I mean we're strong in ourselves because we know what matters and what doesn't. And then it's now. The twenty years have passed and we're just the same. Together, and strong, and happy. And we haven't had to go through all this: we're above it all. It's a stupid dream, isn't it?'

'No. It's not stupid. But it is a dream.'

'Why?'

'Because . . . I don't know, you have to go through it to know what matters and what doesn't. I suppose you have to earn it, don't you? Otherwise . . . well, it's just self-deception.' Whether it helped Sandy, Gordon was unsure. But the realisation certainly helped him.

'Or blissful ignorance.'

'If we'd lived together for the last however many years I'm sure we'd have ended up just the same as we are now. Perhaps even more distant from each other. But this way . . .'

'This way we have a child together. We get on. We don't have to pretend anything. It's just that we're not together.'

'No.'

'So go. Each time I see you it reminds me of the utter mess I'm in. So I don't want you to come here for a while.' Sandy pushed Gordon gently away. He was now sitting back on his heels, his face level with hers, but she was looking at him with a frankness born of new hope.

'I'm sorry,' Gordon said, standing.

'You're always sorry.'

'I know. But this is a different kind of sorry. This is regret, not apology.'

'So you regret it too?'

'Yes. Well, in a way. I don't regret what we had. And I don't regret what I have now. I regret how I've dealt with things. I think, perhaps, I should tell Miranda.'

'Why?'

'Because unless I do, this child will always be a weapon you can use against me.'

'Thanks. That's candid, Gordon. How did you get to be so candid?'

'I don't know. I'm tired of lying.'

'So let me ask you one last time: why did you sleep with Miranda?'

'Because I needed to escape from you.'

'You don't like women very much, do you?'

Miranda was in the bath. Gordon sat on the side with his legs crossed, cradled a glass of Scotch and sweated in the steam as they talked. Miranda's hair was tied back, she had no make-up on, her breasts broke the surface of the soapy water, the rest of her body was hidden.

'How are we doing?' Gordon said.

'How do you think we're doing?' Miranda reached up and Gordon passed her her gin and tonic.

'Alright.'

'Just alright?'

'Better than alright. I went to see Sandy again.'

'Did you?'

'I want to clear something up.'

'With her?'

'With you.'

'Good.' Miranda settled lower in the water.

'I think you already know.'

'Is that an apology?'

'No. It's about the baby.'

'Your baby.'

'Yes. You did know.'

'Well, her baby, really. It is, of course, her baby. You're immaterial. She got what she wanted from you. Piran couldn't give it to her. Clive couldn't either, so she found somebody who could.'

'Well . . .'

'I'm sorry, does that seem harsh? It's not meant to.'

Not only did the loss of Sandy then hit Gordon, but also the realisation that Miranda would never fill the gap.

SIX

'Soooooo,' MONNERY YODELLED the O across the staff room. Jan was away for a few days. His happiness was complete.

'What?' Gordon sat at his feet. His habitual morning confusion was settling into a more tangible despair which, before Monnery had interrupted him, he had been moulding into anger. Anger he could take out on the children he was due to face in a few minutes.

'Soooo. SNAFU. Situation normal . . .'

'Oh shut up, Monnery.' Gordon said. '*Shut the fuck up*,' but this only in his head.

'. . . Normal service has been resumed. God's in his heaven and . . .'

'Normal.' Gordon surfaced. 'Yes, everything is normal. Nothing happened. I might just as well have never left.'

'Except, of course . . .'

'The obvious. Yes. Sandy has a baby. Piran's in the nut house . . .' But it was the rest of it that was troubling Gordon, the ghost of Miranda's lover stalking his happiness, the pointlessness of everything now the gesture of his escape had been made and nothing had come of it, and the lack of anybody to confide in now that Sandy wouldn't see him.

'Miranda seems fine.'

'Does she?'

'Yes, Jan saw her the day before yesterday. She said she seemed very optimistic about things.'

'Good. Bloody marvellous.'

'But you don't,' Monnery accused, then sat down and waited for Gordon to fill him in on the latest developments.

'Don't I? No, I suppose I don't. But then why should I? Dead end job, pushing forty, no shagging prospects, no fucking life, a kid who I can't talk to and a wife who, despite all this, is very optimistic.' Some of this was out loud, but not the bits that mattered. Gordon was afraid that his parallel world would soon spill over into his real world. It was a terrifying prospect, but only in as much as he'd have to confront what he really felt about his circumstances rather than what he pretended to feel. The disparity between the pretence and the reality was widening: an exhausting condition and a marker of his disintegrating mental health.

'I thought things were getting better. I'm sorry, Gordon, if you don't want to talk . . .'

'No. I don't.' *Not to you, anyway. Go fuck yourself, Monnery. Die horribly on the road. Get cancer.*

'Fine.'

'There's nothing to say. I mean, what I had to say I said by leaving. And now I'm back, and nothing's changed. I can't believe that nothing's changed.'

'Between you and Miranda?'

'No, you miss the point.' *You always miss the point.* 'No. Not just that. I mean in me.'

'You're angry. That s changed.'

Fuck fuck fuck off. 'Spare me the farmyard psychology.'

The school bell went. Gordon's shoulders tensed in preparation for the first class of the day.

185

'But what did you want to change?' Monnery said with a passable stab at sympathy.

'I thought . . . oh, I don't know . . .' It was all Monnery deserved. The rest of it, he didn't: *I thought I went because of the guilt. You know, for screwing Sandy. That was somehow easier than apologising and working things out. Just running away and, I don't know, letting Miranda work out what she wanted to do about it. Anyway, she did. She met whatsisname, I came back, suitably chastened, and the slate was wiped clean. We tried again. We tried hard. We tried to make an effort, we tried to see each other's point of view. We even tried to talk things through with some hatchet-faced hag at Relate. But, ultimately, nothing changed. The reasons I slept with Sandy are the same. Because I fancied her. And the reason Miranda had such a good time with whatsisname is the same: she fancied him. And however much we try, the fact is that we just don't do the same for each other. The passion is gone. And when the passion is gone, however much you try, however much you pretend, there will always be something missing. Part of you will be dead . . . that's it. That's all it is.*

Miranda was cooking when Gordon got home. Pen was in the lounge doing her homework and watching the television. Ben was digging a hole in one of the flower beds with a red trowel. The house slumbered contentedly.

'Hello.' Gordon dropped his briefcase onto the floor, went over and Miranda offered her cheek to be kissed. Her skin tasted of salt and perfume.

'Good day?'

'No. You?'

'Alright.'

'What did you do?'

'Oh, I saw Anne, did the washing, made a model with Ben, did the shopping, came back and did the ironing, fetched Pen and took her to her music lesson, fetched her back from her music lesson.' Somewhere there was an accusation, but Gordon didn't have the spirit to take it up.

'Drink?' Gordon waved the bottle of whisky in the air. He was drinking almost a bottle a day.

'No thanks. Later.'

'Jan's away, did you know?'

'Yes.'

'Monnery's unbearable. More unbearable.'

'Her mother's ill.'

'Really?'

'Yes. I don't think she has long.'

'What, Jan?'

'No. Her mother.'

'Right . . . Right. Awful.' It touched him no more than the fact there was barely one decent measure in the whisky bottle. 'Monnery never mentioned it.'

'No. He wouldn't.'

'They make it work though, don't they?'

'What?' Miranda responded to the change in Gordon's tone; an uncharacteristic soberness had crept in.

'Monnery and Jan. Despite it all . . .' Gordon let it go. 'I'll just go and wash.' But he stood for a while and watched Ben carefully turning over the dry soil of the flower bed. The pointlessness of his task was denied by the concentration the child was using.

Gordon went upstairs, sat on the bed, patted his jacket pocket and took out a plastic container of aspirins. He shook the container, opened it, and removed the cotton wool stopper. Then he shook out a palmful of white capsules and looked at them.

'Ten minutes, Pen,' he heard Miranda call.

Pen ate her supper alone in her room. Miranda, Ben and

Gordon sat at the kitchen table. Words were said, but nothing of significance.

'What's the matter?' It was all he heard of Miranda's words; he didn't know how he replied but it seemed to be the answer she was looking for. Ben filled the silence with questions, surreal observations and minor complaints. Afterwards, Gordon carried him upstairs and held him for a while before undressing him and putting him in the bath.

He read Ben two stories then tucked him in to his bed and switched off the light.

'Stay with me,' Ben said from the darkness. Gordon closed the bedroom door and sat on the bed. He stroked the child's forehead.

'It's been morning all day, today,' Ben said. His hand reached out and took Gordon's finger. Soon he was asleep. Gordon lay down beside him and cried for a while. Then he slept too.

PART FOUR

PART FOUR

ONE

'SIT DOWN.' IT was a cautious gesture of welcome. The woman was short and dressed in a black spangled party blouse. She was wearing high heels, her features were East European, her face more suited to intolerance than sympathy. The room had a couch in it with tissue paper placed over the pillow, two high-backed chairs facing each other from a distance of seven or eight feet, a desk, a chimney breast with an unlit fire and three shelves of books. The young woman had had to ring the bell on the gate post, go round to the side of the house and wait to be let in. She had been instructed to arrive no earlier than the appointed time. The meeting felt clandestine.

'How did you come to see me?' The woman's voice was educated and heavily accented.

'You were recommended. I telephoned the register and they gave me your name.'

'Yes . . . so . . . why, then, did you come to see me?' The woman looked at her hands which she had placed in her lap.

The young woman shifted in her chair, crossed her legs, clasped her hands round her knee, waited (because she had been told by a friend not to rush into answers), then said, 'Because I want to understand why I feel like I do.'

'. . . Yes?'

'And I want to know if it's possible to feel differently.'

'You understand that this is a trial session. We will meet, perhaps, twice, and then we will both decide whether you will continue here. Yes?'

'Yes.'

'So tell me how you feel.'

'Desolate.' Having known she would be asked this, the young woman had given the question serious consideration. Desolate conveyed almost completely how she felt.

'Now? Always?'

'Always.'

'And when you talk about desolation, what do you mean by that?'

'I feel . . . cold, and alone. Alone. Just, alone.'

'And are you alone?'

'No. Well, I'm not in any . . . "relationship". I have a brother.'

'Older?'

'No. Younger. We don't see much of each other. My mother tries to push us together but it doesn't work. I mean we're close but we don't need to see each other. We talk on the phone. We're as close as we need to be. I think my mother's afraid we'll end up alone. Like her. But we won't. I mean. I mean we're not into that kind of guilt. She's very . . . Am I talking too much?'

'No. Please go on.'

'She's very guilt ridden. You can't. I can't tell her anything. She won't hear it from me. She blames herself for my father's . . . well, I suppose that's why I'm here. My father.'

'Yes?'

'He left us. Well, he left us once before. He went to Egypt with a man called Professor Bunyan. Not really. He wasn't really called. That's how I, I mean, that's what . . . Anyway, I knew where he. But I made him come back, and I don't think he . . . was quite ready. So my mother is not the guilty one. I think it was . . . I think it was my fault. But I loved my father dearly. Dearly. Love him. Still. And I miss him. Everybody misses him. But I think when he . . . it was a kind of a mistake, really. Because I think he felt he. I think he felt unique. But he wasn't.'

'He wasn't unique.'

'I think we're similar. He and I. I think we see the world in the same way. I don't want to end up like him. I don't want to die. I don't want to die a virgin. I'm twenty years old. He's been gone for nearly ten years and I can't bear anybody touching me. Does that seem? I'm not saying. No. I don't think. Look, I mean I don't want to end up like him. But I want to understand why he did what he did. That's all. I want to understand him. I wish I could talk to him.'

'Do you talk to him?'

'In what way? Do you mean do I pray? No, I don't pray, I don't have any religious beliefs. It's ridiculous really, isn't it? I mean people always tell me how capable I am. I don't feel capable. But the question is, isn't it, what I want to say to him, that's the question you're asking isn't it . . . and the truth is that I don't know. Except to say the most obvious things, but, perhaps it's the obvious things you never say . . . Daddy, I love you. And I miss you. God I miss you. He killed himself you see. For no good reason we could think of. Except he couldn't find a good enough reason not to. And I know he didn't mean to do it, otherwise . . . otherwise he would have left a note. Wouldn't he?'

Chris Paling

AFTER THE RAID

'Haunting, intense and enviably accomplished'
Nick Hornby

'During the Blitz, a German bombing raid on London leaves
Gregory Swift shell-shocked and disorientated. He travels to
Manchester to visit his sister, but the train is diverted and he
finds himself in the company of a schoolboy and a nurse,
exploring an unreal, almost deserted English village. Or is
this another hallucination?...This is an unusual and unsettling book which not only summons up ghostly memories of
our recent history, but also delivers a gentle kick in the pants
to the "realistic" assumptions of English fiction'
Mail on Sunday

'An impressive feat of historical imagining'
Independent

'Part of the book's haunting power is due to the beautifully
crafted opening pages...They alone justify the cost of the
book...The creation of suspense through such laconic
writing reminds one of Graham Greene'
Literary Review

V

VINTAGE

Chris Paling

DESERTERS

'Among the most accomplished English novelist to emerge
in recent years'
Independent

'Cliffie, an amoral, sexually meandering misanthrope,
deserts his histrionic partner Barry to take flight with their
unhinged flatmate May in a bid to save her from institution-
alisation...These people also serve to help Paling explore the
nature of relationships – what we need from them, what we
owe to them and suggest that their final value can never be
foreseen...Gripping stuff'
Time Out

'A strangely compelling read...There's a raw energy at work
here...the narrative rattles along at a breathless pace'
Literary Review

VINTAGE

Alan Warner

MORVERN CALLAR

'A dazzling achievement...he defines the 90s as clearly as Ian
McEwan defined the 70s and Jay McInerney the 80s'
Time Out

It is off-season in a remote Highland sea-port: 21-year-old
Morvern Callar, a low-paid employee in the local supermar-
ket, wakes one morning to find her strange boyfriend has
committed suicide and is dead on their kitchen floor.
Morvern's laconic reaction is both intriguing and immoral.
What she does next is even more appalling...

'Bleak, haunting and brilliantly original'
Nick Hornby

'Morvern gleams like an onyx from a vivid, macabre and
lyrical book...she is impossible to forget'
Guardian

'Morvern is a brilliant creation...more than a stunning debut
novel; to my mind it establishes Alan Warner as one of the
most talented, original and interesting voices around'
Irvine Welsh

VINTAGE

Also available in Vintage

Alan Warner

THESE DEMENTED LANDS

'Prodigious powers of invention...marvellously dynamic prose...brilliant visual imagination...A greatly ambitious novel'
Times Literary Supplement

'A sequel to his acclaimed debut novel, *Morvern Callar*, *These Demented Lands* confirms that Alan Warner boasts an extravagant talent...This novel is set on a Scottish island that contains a variety of weird landmarks and an hallucinogenic cast of characters including a DJ who wants to set up the rave to end all raves, a visitor whose job it is to assess candidates for sainthood, and the wonderfully unfazed heroine, Morvern Callar'
Mail on Sunday

'A novel that follows the trajectory of the drug trip: luminous, hallucinatory and utterly illogical. There is unlikely to be a more original, or hysterically imagined, book published this year'
The Times

'Warner's second novel is a classic like his first one... glorious...powerful'
Independent on Sunday

V

VINTAGE

Ann-Marie MacDonald

FALL ON YOUR KNEES

*Winner of the 1997 Commonwealth
Writers Prize for Best First Book*

'An epic in the true sense: a magnificent novel...It is the
unpredictability of this huge book that is its greatest joy'
Philippa Gregory, *Sunday Times*

Following the curves of the twentieth century, *Fall on your
Knees* takes us from haunted Cape Breton Island in Nova
Scotia through the battlefields of World War I into the
emerging jazz scene of New York City, and immerses us in
the lives of four unforgettable sisters.

'Extraordinary...*Fall on your Knees* has all the qualities of a
nightmarish fairy tale...A magical tale, a curious testament
to both the power of love and the inability of humans to live
fully without it'
Mary Loudon, *The Times*

'A heady, haunting brew, carefully structured, witty and
distinctive'
Christina Patterson, *Observer*

VINTAGE

A SELECTED LIST OF CONTEMPORARY FICTION
AVAILABLE IN VINTAGE

☐ CANDY	Luke Davies	£5.99
☐ BIRDSONG	Sebastian Faulks	£6.99
☐ THE FOLDING STAR	Alan Hollinghurst	£6.99
☐ FALL ON YOUR KNEES	Ann-Marie MacDonald	£6.99
☐ THE CONVERSATIONS AT CURLOW CREEK	David Malouf	£5.99
☐ REMEMBERING BABYLON	David Malouf	£6.99
☐ THE GIANT'S HOUSE	Elizabeth McCracken	£5.99
☐ I WAS AMELIA EARHART	Jane Mendelsohn	£5.99
☐ SELECTED STORIES	Alice Munro	£6.99
☐ AFTER THE RAID	Chris Paling	£5.99
☐ DESERTERS	Chris Paling	£5.99
☐ IN A FATHER'S PLACE	Christopher Tilghman	£5.99
☐ MASON'S RETREAT	Christopher Tilghman	£5.99
☐ LADDER OF YEARS	Anne Tyler	£5.99
☐ MORVERN CALLAR	Alan Warner	£5.99
☐ THESE DEMENTED LANDS	Alan Warner	£5.99

- All Vintage books are available through mail order or from your local bookshop.

- Please send cheque/eurocheque/postal order (sterling only), Access, Visa or Mastercard:

☐☐☐☐☐☐☐☐☐☐☐☐☐☐☐☐

Expiry Date:_____Signature:_____

Please allow 75 pence per book for post and packing U.K.
Overseas customers please allow £1.00 per copy for post and packing.

ALL ORDERS TO:

Vintage Books, Book Service by Post, P.O.Box 29, Douglas, Isle of Man, IM99 1BQ.
Tel: 01624 675137 • Fax: 01624 670923

NAME:_____

ADDRESS:_____

_____

_____

Please allow 28 days for delivery. Please tick box if you do not
wish to receive any additional information   ☐

Prices and availability subject to change without notice.